SECURITY BREACH

Scouting along the underground passage way, Eli Franklin stumbled on another opening leading even deeper into the covert stronghold. He climbed down several levels until he hit bottom, and stopped to listen.

Nothing.

It was pitch black in the metallic maze of corridors, and he had to grope his way forward. That's when the walls started humming. The farther in he went, the louder the humming became. He started to walk faster, then run.

The ceiling exploded in red light. The humming transformed into the shriek of a security alarm. Two men wearing masks closed on him.

Petrified, he reached for a terrifying weapon of his own.

THE BLACK HOLE AFFAIR

JEFFREY KLEIN

ZEBRA BOOKS
KENSINGTON PUBLISHING CORP.

For Judith, lodestar

ZEBRA BOOKS

are published by

Kensington Publishing Corp.
475 Park Avenue South
New York, NY 10016

First printing: August, 1991

Printed in the United States of America

Author's Note

The Black Hole Affair grew out of a year's reporting throughout Silicon Valley. In the high-tech capital of the United States, some 60,000 employees have security clearances to work on the Pentagon's classified projects. Many of these people create in the dark: their salaries come from the $35 billion a year the Defense Department has buried in its black budget; their subsystems combine into weapons whose ultimate aims and abilities they are forbidden to know.

A shorter version of this novel was first serialized in Silicon Valley's newspaper of record, *The San Jose Mercury News*. No factual objections have ever surfaced.

Prologue

December 1988

Mr. Williams' expressionless gaze was disturbing.

Andy Lamkin turned to wave to his baby daughter Dolores, propped in her portable car seat at the foot of his chair. The floor seemed safer than the restaurant's glass-covered table.

OK, bringing Dolores along had been a little unprofessional. But her presence also showed that his research project was impoverished. The days his wife worked, Andy couldn't afford a baby-sitter. Besides, Dolores was amusing herself nicely with the clutch ball, the plastic chopsticks and the soup ladle Andy successively awarded her.

"How many other people work with you?" asked Mr. Williams.

"Just me. When I was a graduate student at Stanford, a few friends helped out. But nowadays everyone seems to have lost interest."

"Well, I'm interested," Mr. Williams said.

"You can't imagine how much I appreciate that." In a decade when grant money had evaporated, Mr.

Williams' New World Peace Institute had actually approached Andy. "You know, I'm familiar with the Institute for Policy Studies in Washington, but before you called, I'd never heard of your organization."

"We're a much quieter group," Mr. Williams said, neatly folding back his shirtsleeves. "We just fund promising work. Anonymously. Tell me: What investigations are you pursuing now?"

"The military's secret push into space. They already feel they can win any war by immediately controlling the skies."

"Then what's the push?"

"To extend their domination beyond the atmosphere and into the future."

"Are you speculating?"

"Well, the Star Wars subcontracts that I've documented show that we're up to far more than we admit."

"Isn't Star Wars gearing down along with the Cold War?" Mr. Williams said while deskewering his last stick of grilled aromatic beef. "Hasn't it lost credibility?"

"You don't have to believe in Star Wars to build it. If the military-industrial complex just gets prototype weapons aloft, they can attack the public treasury."

A wince? Did Andy see Mr. Williams suppress one? Phrases like "military-industrial complex" made Andy self-conscious. Even among friends he felt like the California Indian Ishi, the last speaker of a doomed language.

"How do you collect your aerospace data?" Mr. Williams asked with continuing directness.

" 'Data' makes my work sound too glamorous. I'm probably the only person in Silicon Valley who can't afford a computer. I just clip and file information, mostly from defense industry newsletters."

"And who uses this information?"

Andy toyed with the last vegetables in his firepot and wondered if he should beef up his customer base. His wife, Inez, was always criticizing him for underselling. But Andy was a born Quaker. "Not too many people, to be honest. A few reporters, a couple of foreign news services. I'm primarily an archivist. Sometimes I feel as if we're living in Detroit in the 1950s, and everyone's agreed not to mention the word 'car.' "

"Something wrong with cars? Are you anti-everything?"

"Well," Andy said sheepishly, "a comparable investment in mass transportation would have been wiser. But I agree with you—cars and interstate highways catalyzed America's economy. The money siphoned off into these secret weapons should be spent renovating our infrastructure, don't you think?"

"Not my area of expertise. Tell me: When you're collecting information, do you ever get any walk-in intelligence? Any clandestine tips?"

Andy looked around the Quoc Te, which was alive with Vietnamese enjoying their own conversations. At last, he thought to himself, a selling point! "Well just a couple of weeks ago, I got a call from a woman who wanted to tip me off about one weapons program she said would survive the Cold War."

"Did she give you any details?" Mr. Williams leaned forward. "Any names?"

9

"She mentioned somebody named William Powell. Or Wilson Powers. To tell you the truth, I'm terrible with names. I told her if she could provide some technical or budget information, I'd follow up."

Mr. Williams pressed the tips of his fingers together. "Well, you've certainly provided . . ."

A husky Asian man toting a shopping bag bumped into their table. Herbs rained down on the baby. Andy and the Asian man immediately bent down to see if Dolores was hurt. Mr. Williams fiddled with the drip filters atop his and Andy's Vietnamese coffees.

Dolores was, if anything, entertained.

When the commotion settled and the shopping bag was repacked, Mr. Williams lifted up his Cafe Sua Nong and proposed a toast. "Let's drink to the future! I'm going to recommend you get all the funding you deserve."

Andy wasn't a coffee drinker. His idea of stimulation was reading *Aviation Week* while sipping chamomile tea. But Mr. Williams had proudly ordered this Vietnamese specialty for both of them and the occasion seemed to call for male bonding.

After the toast, Mr. Williams stood up and extended his hand. "I'll get back to you in a week. Remember: Keep our meeting confidential. My institute's angels insist on total anonymity. Don't even discuss our conversation with your wife."

Since Mr. Williams had ignored the baby during lunch, Andy was surprised when he bent down to kiss her on the forehead before leaving.

In his wake Mr. Williams left two $20 bills on the table. The check hadn't even arrived! Andy raised

Dolores up by her seat and said, "Honey, welcome to Fat City!"

Andy's 1974 Peugeot was parked in the adjacent lot. He snapped the bolted anchor strap onto the back of Dolores' car seat, then snugly fastened the regular belt across her waist. He joined 101 near the San Jose airport and headed toward his office, which was in the garage adjacent to his tiny home in Mountain View, the poor man's Palo Alto.

As he passed Moffett Field, an old navy plane zoomed directly across the freeway before landing. The prop jet looked like a relic from a World War II movie. But Andy knew that the magnetic anomaly detector sticking out in back was a telltale: these planes had been retrofitted with the most advanced electronic equipment available. They could cruise for hours scanning for Soviet submarines offshore. They could even invade enemy radar to detect how their own threat was perceived, then alter their apparent location and profile. Their old gray skins were really sophisticated camouflage.

Andy inspected the skin on the back of his hands, then looked at his palms. They were glistening with sweat.

He regripped the steering wheel in what seemed like slow motion. The drive home seemed to be stretching out. He stared at the speedometer. "Fifty," he said aloud. The sound seemed to take fifty seconds to reach his ears.

His body felt so rubbery. He flexed his arms and legs as if they were rubber bands. "Twaanngg, twaanngg, twaanngg," he heard himself say.

In the back seat Dolores smiled, thinking her

daddy was singing to her.

Andy didn't notice because he'd closed his eyes. Amazing! With his eyes shut, he could see himself driving and twaanngging.

Probably he should open his eyes and pull off the freeway. He could hear his heart ba-booommnnngg in his chest. Was it really pounding or had he just never listened this carefully?

When he opened his eyes, his heartbeat swelled. Friends often said he was big-hearted. His father-in-law worried that he was a soft-heart — a *corazón blando*.

He started to pull over. A car smacked his right rear. Had he forgotten to check his blind spot? He watched himself panic while fighting to regain control of his rubbery limbs.

His Peugeot twisted into the fast lane, where it was smashed broadside by another car. The Peugeot flipped over and the black steering wheel crushed Andy's chest.

Strange at such a moment to remember a poem: "I Am Going to Speak of Hope." The César Vallejo poster was in his bathroom at home. All the verses spoke about suffering the world's pain. Why that hopeful title?

After two-and-a-half flips, the Peugeot came to a rest upside down on the freeway's shoulder. A motorist in a Mercedes passing the other way used a cellular phone to report the accident. An ambulance and three Highway Patrol cars arrived within five minutes.

Dolores was hanging upside down, wailing more out of fear than pain. It took an eternity to dislodge her. Then the men went through the professional motions with Andy.

The wreckage was cleared before the afternoon commute. Only shards remained, but for a while traffic slowed around the accident site as if the freeway itself had been traumatized. By dark, however, all cars resumed their pace.

When the autopsy results came in, the Highway Patrol officer wasn't surprised. He'd seen that kind of grin before, though never as a death mask. This fool Lamkin had been so loaded on PCP and speed, he probably couldn't have walked a foot unaided.

1

A Brilliance in the Night

January 1989

Before the countdown reached four, Eli felt a fearsome rumble — as if 100,000 sports cars were revving their engines.

"What if it's a no-go?" he thought. "Can we abort in four seconds?"

Three, two, one . . . Ignition!

Ferocious orange flames burst from the rocket, thrusting the 20-story missile off its pad. What a coup! He'd witnessed the secret launch of the century! The five-pointed star on the fading fuselage was just like the decals he'd stuck on his model fighter planes as a kid. He nodded knowingly to Andy Lamkin, who was sharing his bunker.

Was Lamkin his guide or assistant? He had to know because . . . the rocket's guidance system had gone haywire! The fucking missile was heading back toward the ground! He turned again to ask Lamkin, who was now pockmarked with purple measles. Lamkin smiled at Eli; his gums were bleeding.

15

"They'll claim it's a routine satellite launch," Lamkin said. "They're worse liars than I imagined."

When the missile hit, a phenomenal white light illuminated Lamkin's bones.

Eli should run away. The missile blasted into the earth, shaking the ground beneath him madly. He had to run away, he had to run. . .

When he awoke, the bed was rattling. Must be an earthquake, his first California quake.

He threw off the quilt. No time to worry about clothes. This had to be more than a seven. Maybe California's big one. Running out the door, he noticed nothing else in the house was shaking. If this was the big one, wouldn't some lamps have fallen? At least a book or two?

Eli found himself alone on the mountaintop. The January night was utterly still. Three other houses were within sight, but no lights were on in any of them. Why no commotion?

He gazed up at the sky. Streaking across it was a radiant white light shaped like an arrowhead. Bright blue flames shot out of its tail. It was too big to be a meteor, too fast for an airplane.

As the incandescent object darted across the heavens, a neighborhood dog started to howl. Hadn't Eli read that quakes rattled animals?

The howl changed into snarls. A German shepherd was racing up the hill toward him. He'd seen this nasty dog every time he'd turned up Old Preacher's Road. Eli looked down. He was just wearing underpants. It was the middle of the night. The barking would awaken his neighbors, who'd see him standing outside, semi-naked, cornered. He

16

picked up a handful of pebbles and hurled them at the dog as he retreated inside.

He turned on his cabin's lights. Nothing was askew. His digital clock read 1:13. If there had been even a momentary interruption in the power supply, it would have been flashing 12:00. The German shepherd let loose a wretched howl, then drifted down the hill.

Eli phoned the San Jose police to see if anyone else had felt an earthquake. A beep went off in the background to let him know that his call was being recorded.

"No one else has reported anything yet," the cop on duty said. "Would you like to leave your name and address?"

Eli knew his phone number was automatically displayed on the officer's screen. Did they think he was some kind of nut?

"No, thank you, Officer," Eli said ever so politely. "My wife's just nervous about this sort of thing. We've only been out in California a few weeks. Maybe we had a little foundation slippage. I'll check on it tomorrow morning."

After hanging up, Eli taunted himself: "My imaginary wife—is she married to an East Coast paranoid?"

He couldn't get back to sleep. At 5:40, he heard the first delivery van drive up the hill and toss a paper outside his door. His beloved *New York Times*. He fetched it and foraged through it, but it contained no news of the night. He knew it wouldn't. This national edition had gone to bed earlier than he had. Soon the *Wall Street Journal*

17

and the *San Jose Mercury News* flung their missiles on his doorstep. Nothing in them, either. He turned on the local radio stations — late-breaking earthquakes were their cup of news. No luck. Inane disc jockeys were prattling to take everyone's mind off the morning commute.

"Idiots!" he shouted, wishing he were back home in Manhattan.

On his dresser was a kind of New York souvenir — this year's National Magazine Award, an abstract rendering of an elephant. He picked up the metal sculpture and caught sight of himself in the bedroom mirror. On a whim, he placed the sculpture atop his curly red hair. Was the trophy too small or Eli's head too large? In either case, the crown didn't fit.

Eli had won the award for four *Newsweek* profiles: "My Problems With the Boss," "Tom Wolfe's Big Bad Secret," "Why Dr. Huxtable Isn't Delivering" and "Is *60 Minutes* Running out of Time?" With a comic flair for exposing hypocrisy, Eli had composed pretentious rock poetry about Springsteen, satirized Wolfe, ribbed Cosby, investigated Mike Wallace. Eli had a knack for joining with his subjects so that they naturally revealed themselves. Mike Wallace hadn't even realized afterward that he'd been shown naked. Which was just as well, because to play in *Newsweek*, these pieces had to celebrate what they were criticizing.

In his acceptance remarks at the Waldorf, Eli had turned the tables, castigating the celebration. "While I'm grateful for your recognition, I'm troubled by the cowardice I feel infecting our industry.

We seem to be lost in a funhouse of celebrity covers. Or is it a whorehouse? We pride ourselves on copulating exclusively with megastars who agree to reveal nothing. Meanwhile prophetic voices are going unheard and visionaries unseen."

The reception was the worst imaginable: faint applause. Now as Eli reconsidered his motives for the fiftieth time, a filler in the back pages of the State News section of the local paper leaped out at him as if it were a 500-point headline.

"UFO Scare in S. Cal.," it said. "Dozens of San Luis Obispo residents called the police last night to report what appeared to be a brilliant UFO streaking across the sky. Vandenberg Air Force Base confirmed that at approximately 1 A.M. they'd made a routine launch." End of item.

At least Eli hadn't hallucinated. But when he pulled out a California map, he found that San Luis Obispo was only a few miles from Vandenberg Air Force Base, some 250 miles to the south. How could he have seen a missile from so far away? And more: How could he have imagined the damned launch in his dream?

He stroked his throat with his thumb and forefinger. Right after the gala awards luncheon, he'd succumbed to a flu. He felt congested for too long a time. He lost his voice, his appetite, his energy. No food seemed appealing, nobody worth profiling. The "witty, incisive" style the judges cited made Eli fret his work had become formulaic. Refried celebrities and parboiled cultural insights covered with a citric glaze.

His editor assigned him to cover the John Lennon controversy brewing in Manhattan. *People* was about to run prepublication excerpts of Goldman's nasty biography; *Rolling Stone* planned to retaliate by disparaging the author's key sources. Eli understood his mission: Justify *Newsweek*'s desire to put Lennon's salable face on its cover; summarize the best gossip up high in the story; but chide both cynics and idolaters for their excesses.

The article he wrote in a night disturbed him. Exploiting dead stars felt like a blasphemous step beyond the pale, as if he'd memorialized Lennon with a lounge version of "Imagine."

Afterward Eli proposed "getting out into the country"—lingua Manhattan for any travel outside the Big Island. A working title for his proposed piece sprang to mind: "America's Secret Dreams for the 21st Century."

Talk about gassy! But he wanted to be vague at the outset so that he could report what he'd actually discovered instead of prejudging from a skyscraper that stared resentfully at other glass buildings. His own view from the southwest flank of *Newsweek*'s building was being obliterated by a new high rise. The girder crew was already at work right outside his tenth floor window. Sayonara Rockefeller Center.

"I'll spend a couple of months with real people in suburban California," he told his editor, "and analyze their *Weltanschauung.*"

"Heavy stuff," his editor had said. "You wouldn't be trying to spend a sunny winter with your older brother?"

"I'm not proposing a retreat to America's womb.

20

I'll tell you what: I'll throw in my own vacation. I haven't taken any real time off in two years."

Time off—Eli had little left. He called the public information office down at Vandenberg. "Last night, where was that rocket heading?"

The officer in charge said he'd get back shortly. Was Eli in New York City or at a bureau?

"I'm on special assignment in California. Doing a few fruits-and-nuts stories. I'm working out of my house, but you'll find my name on the *Newsweek* masthead under 'Senior Writers.' And if you misplace my number, just ask the 408 operator for Los Gatos. I've rented a cabin in an unincorporated area atop the Santa Cruz Mountains."

From a previous journalistic incarnation, Eli understood this game—standard military procedure for checking if a reporter was who he claimed to be.

A half hour later, when the Vandenberg lieutenant colonel called back, Eli acted cavalier. "So this rocket that was mistaken for a UFO, does that happen often?"

"More than you'd think. When fuel and water vapor freeze in the upper atmosphere, they reflect sunlight from beneath the horizon. We're probably responsible for a majority of the UFO rumors on the West Coast. That's just a guess, mind you. I have no hard figures on that."

"So from your perspective, what was unusual about this launch?"

"Nothing at all."

"And the payload was?"

"A weather satellite."

21

"No kidding. What kind?"

"Well, because the satellite has some minor military capabilities, I can't provide details."

"Can you tell me off the record?"

"Off the record and not for attribution?"

"You have my word."

"I really shouldn't be telling you this, but most of our weather satellites can be used as backups in case any of our surveillance vehicles fail. If it's an overcast night, for instance, the Global Protection Network might temporarily need an extra pair of eyes."

"For what?"

"To peer through the clouds. That's all I'm prepared to say."

Eli couldn't extract any more information, though he felt the officer was shining him on. The rocket in his dreams was at least 20 stories tall. It was lifting something titanic.

"A couple of final questions — trivial ones, really. I'm just trying to picture the launch in my mind. It helps me write my lead."

"Go ahead, shoot."

"What kind of decal did the rocket have on it?"

"Decal? You mean identification?"

"Yes, you know, like a flag."

"The major identification on these Titans is the Air Force Star. That must be why you said 'decal.' Yes, it looks like the star on toy models."

"No kidding. And could you give me a sense of the rocket's power in terms an average *Newsweek* reader might understand — say, compared to a sports car?"

"Well, let's assume the average sports car has 200 horsepower. So, 1.6 million pounds of thrust translates into 100,000 cars."

"Unbelievable."

"Not really. Just a routine launch."

Eli hung up. It wasn't a dream; it was a nightmare. And what was Andy Lamkin doing soothsaying in it? Eli hadn't received one of Lamkin's earnest, semi-paranoid newsletters for God knows how long.

2

The Call

To flush the dream from his system, Eli stretched his daily run to 10 miles. So far, his main accomplishment in California was blazing an ever-lengthening course of mountain paths. Ten miles! Jogging his standard four around the crowded Central Park Reservoir, Eli would occasionally nod to the disguised Jackie O, whom he'd met twice at Doubleday book parties.

A steep fire trail now rose amid the firs before him. Fatigued from sleeping fitfully, he closed his eyes and chugged ahead. He saw the missile blasting into the ground.

Back in his cabin, he poured himself a bowl of oat bran flakes. In Manhattan, he was always wrestling with his appetite in the finest gravy. *Newsweek*'s generous policy on expenses transformed every midtown menu into a free smorgasbord. Four pounds one year, five the next—soon Eli weighed in at 220, which had filled out his six-three frame but bloated his baby face.

Now, in six weeks, he'd lost 24 pounds! He sprinkled some raisins onto his oat bran and con-

24

tinued eating. The raisins looked cute, almost as if they were dimples in a face smiling at him. Or purple pustules. He saw the measled Lamkin with bleeding gums.

He retired to work in the bedroom, whose picture window overlooked a redwood forest. In this bedroom, he'd stationed his computer and his calling cards—two enormous, circular Rolodexes that looked like fighting vehicles from *Star Wars*. Hundreds of sources were arranged alphabetically on one. On the other, duplicates of the same cards had been rearranged under subject headings: art, books, lifestyle, media, movies, music, newsmakers, pop shrinks, sports, television, theater, trends.

"Back of the Book" categories. That's how everyone at *Newsweek* referred to the sections where Eli worked. The phrase's accuracy intensified Eli's loathing of it. He couldn't stand the cheerful "Back of the Book" sign that greeted him each time he exited from the elevator onto his floor. He was insulted by the reception desk's accordion folder whose pleats bore "Back of the Book" labels. Each day his superiors two floors up would send down "FYI" into this folder lifestyle, media or newsmaker stories that they'd clipped. As if Eli couldn't read the *Times!*

Eli now scanned through his subject cards, which he'd color-coded by location, Big Apple Red dominating. He flipped through the goldenrods searching for Northern California names. His visionary essay about America's secret dreams was . . . was . . . unrealistic. Leave it at that. He'd do one quick celebrity profile, cut his losses and head home.

25

Cruz Smith, Gold, Mitford and Steel under books; Coppola, Lucas and Zaentz under movies; Baez, Fogerty, Garcia and Lewis under music. His Rolodex's reach beyond Manhattan was pathetic, but Northern California didn't seem to be holding up its end, either. Mostly flashes from the past. He dialed Joan Baez's number.

"Hello. Hello."

It was her voice, she'd answered her own phone. He hung up. He had nothing new to say about Baez.

He grabbed his other Rolodex and flipped to the L's. The faded Lamkin card was more than a decade old. He pounded out the number.

"This is Inez," the recording said. "Dolorescita and I have gone south to stay with my family. I don't know when we'll return, but leave a message if you care to."

When the beep sounded, Eli hesitated: "Hi . . . this is Eli Franklin. Andy's old freshman roommate. I've . . . been out of touch for a while. Hope I've gotten the right number. If I have, could you ask Andy to ring me back at 555-7810?"

As soon as Eli hung up, he figured: Inez was Lamkin's wife's name, but she didn't even mention him; her tone had a bitter tinge; they're probably divorced.

Then he mocked himself: "Out of touch for a while!" Typical reporter crap! Eli hadn't returned Lamkin's last couple of phone calls.

Assigned as freshman roommates, they'd been friendly enough. Eli respected the way Andy spent his extracurricular time tutoring kids in Harlem.

Eli was himself caught up in his final stretch of athletic stardom. All State in high school with high College Board scores, he'd been recruited to play on Columbia's basketball team.

They'd slept three linoleumed feet apart for one year, but never been that close. "Buzz off!" Eli now shouted and flung his pillow across the room. It struck and rattled the picture window.

Why was he so pissed about a dumb dream and a routine launch that didn't concern him?

The days were ticking away. Eli was due back in New York. He had zilch to show.

One afternoon he ran 15 miles along the very top of the ridge. The winter's gray light was fading—he couldn't exactly see the Pacific. He imagined a line on the featureless horizon where the coast probably ended and the ocean began.

What was so bad about a one-season failure? Surely, after all his successes, *Newsweek* owed him a risk that didn't work out. But at risk, he feared, was something more precious. If he turned away from his suspicions about the rocket launch, if he returned to a life of middlebrow pseudocriticism, would he ever venture into the unknown again? Would he ever snare what was bugging him?

As he jogged up to his cabin, he heard the phone ringing. He couldn't reach it in time. While showering, he thought he heard someone knocking. He wrapped himself in a towel and hurried to the front door. No one was there.

The next day, he drove down to Sunnyvale for a

final visit with his brother's family. Fred had gone to San Jose State, where he'd met Faith. After 20 years of marriage, they had three almost-grown boys.

When Eli arrived, his nephews slapped him flying fives. "D-day, Unc!" said the oldest, anticipating their final game.

"You mean Mayday, pipsqueaks!" Eli teased these kids as if they were his own. Because he feared he couldn't provide enough security (despite all evidence to the contrary), Eli planned not to have kids of his own.

At the playground, he played alone as a one-man team, but found himself uncharacteristically out of focus. While wondering what stars had in common, a rebound bounced off of his head. Despite popular demand, most stars weren't charming people leading charmed lives. They were the driven wounded, paid handsomely to distract us from . . . An errant pass between his nephews struck him full-face.

Soon the score was tied at 18 apiece. He felt the preignition rumbling and saw the missile fire upward. Gravity be damned, Eli soared over his nephews' heads for the winning dunk.

"Next year," he graciously told his young opponents, "I'll be a dead man."

Then he couldn't get those words out of his head.

Before dinner, he took his brother aside and confided, "Did I ever tell you that right before Daddy died, I kept swimming laps back and forth under water? And while I was swimming, I had a feeling that my whole world was about to change for the worse."

"You mentioned that to me years ago," Fred reassured him. "But I'm sure you were tipped off by people staring at you. The grown-ups at the club knew he was dead before they told us. You picked up clues."

No. The adults' patronizing whispers only confirmed what Eli already knew. Diving under the water, he'd felt primitive, amphibian. His father would die while teeing off, and Eli would enter another world. Two new worlds: the adult world, prematurely; and the underwater world that adults never talked about, even in whispers.

During dinner, Eli cracked fewer jokes than usual. As he was leaving to drive back up the Santa Cruz Mountains, Fred hugged him, then warned: "Now don't do anything that will get my little brother in trouble."

One night later, Eli got the troublesome phone call he was awaiting. He'd gone to sleep early. His ritualistic dissection of the late news had been preempted by Inaugural specials. He had drowsed off when the phone rang. The muffled female voice on the other end of the line asked, "Are you the reporter from *Newsweek* who's been asking about rocket launches?"

"Yes," he said.

"You're on to something big. The weapon they're hatching is more monstrous than you can imagine."

"What is it?"

"Ask Wilson Powers. He works in your valley."

The phrase—"your valley"—caught Eli's ear. "Where do you work?" he asked.

"Not with Powers, but I am in a position to know."

"Where can I meet you? Any place, any time."

"Much too dangerous. He's a killer. Don't let his plainness fool you. Please: Don't mention me when you reach him."

"Can I . . ." Eli started to ask.

But the caller hung up.

3

General Powers

Wilson Powers seemed to be everywhere and nowhere. Many people Eli called in the valley had heard Powers' name, but no one could recall exactly for whom he worked. At least that's what they claimed.

Eli needed to stretch his investigative muscles. In the '70s, he'd been a promising muckraker. His *Village Voice* series on "The Network of Greed: New York's Fiscal Speculators" had won so many prizes, Eli had been certain that the *New York Times* would come calling with a job offer. It didn't.

But one day *Newsweek*'s new editor-in-chief, courtly Bill Broyles, phoned to ask if Eli would "help usher in an era that will put magazine writing back into newsmagazines, but be tougher than *Time*." Eli leaped. More than he ever let on, he loved the swollen salary, the taxi chits, the free researchers, the subsidized cafeteria, the returned phone calls, the expense account questioned when he didn't spend enough. Yet before Eli could prove his worth, Broyles was ushered out.

Eli was sent to the Back of the Book where he

couldn't do much harm. Quickly he learned two tricks about covering popular culture. One: Write about whatever's most popular. Two: Don't be too cultured.

Like other talented writers of his generation, Eli turned his analytic eye to celebrities. His editors never told him to stop digging or to avoid downers, they just brightened when he pitched famous names. The same handwriting was on every magazine's cover. *Rolling Stone* segued into *Us*. *Esquire* slipped unabashedly into *GQ*'s clothes. Eli cursed his calling when PR agents would routinely deny access, then bargain about the conditions under which their clients just might "participate." But gradually he cultivated enough inroads and enough of a reputation that few agents dared deny him.

In his attempts to pinpoint Wilson Powers in Silicon Valley, the *Newsweek* connection got Eli's calls answered. But the pulse was weak. These executives and engineers didn't yearn to join Eli's world. Fundamentally, they didn't care about . . . well, the public notice everyone in Manhattan and D.C. and L.A. craved.

So how had the woman tipster located Eli in the first place? From his initial phone call to Vandenberg? Word had probably been passed to Wilson Powers to beware of Eli—and someone along the way, someone angry but afraid, had decided to give Eli a whiff of the prey. Eli called Vandenberg again and asked to speak with Wilson Powers.

"Major General Powers?" the operator asked.

"Yes," Eli said, elated.

"Oh, he left here a couple of years ago."

"That's terrible. Willie and I went to high school eons ago and now I'm in charge of our reunion. I'm sure he'd want to come. Where do you think I could reach him?"

"I remember something about the redwoods. Redwoods, California. I believe he entered the private sector there."

Eli could find no listing for Redwoods, Calif. He checked directory assistance in Redwood City, Redwood Estates and Redwood Valley. Then Redway, Redlands, Redding, Red Bluff. No luck. Fifty permutations and false leads later, he called Redwood Partners in Menlo Park.

"Excuse me," he asked, "does a Wilson Powers work there?"

"General Powers is the managing partner."

"Great. Can I speak with him?"

Redwood Partners' receptionist was courteous, but sturdy. She said General Powers wasn't in this afternoon; then wasn't in today; then was out of town for the week. Each time Eli called, she apologized for not getting back previously, then asked him for more information so that she could perhaps help.

"Could I tell General Powers who recommended that you see him?" she asked.

"Well, I spoke with them off the record so I'd rather not say. But tell General Powers I'll guarantee him the same anonymity. I'm not looking for quotes, just insight and background."

Several phone calls later, Eli's persistence paid off. He was offered a half-hour appointment at an address on Sand Hill Road. The receptionist told

33

him the office's exact location in a corner on the second story. When he arrived at the modest building facing a suburban courtyard, he understood why her directions had been so explicit. Redwood Partners' name wasn't listed on the entrance directory, nor on their front door. He knocked and noticed a small camera peering down at him from the eaves. The door clicked open. The receptionist was seated behind her desk, literally blocking the way into the office. She was a youngish Japanese woman whose black hair hung to her waist.

"You're so pretty," Eli said charmingly when he greeted her. "All this time we were talking on the phone, I never imagined you'd be this pretty."

She gave a hint of a blush and Eli asked, "What's your name?"

"Miss Tanaka. Yuriko Tanaka."

Miss Tanaka offered him the lone chair in the corner that passed for a reception area. When she soon ushered him into General Powers' windowless, thick-doored compartment, Eli saw no other offices, no other way in or out.

General Powers sat sans jacket with his white shirtsleeves neatly rolled up. He was younger than Eli had expected, perhaps 45. And intensely lean— his elbows, cheekbones, even his raccoonish eye sockets stuck out.

"I've been hearing about you," General Powers said.

"Good things, I hope."

"Contradictory things. What kind of story are you working on?"

"Well, several stories. Our company likes to get the most out of its workers."

The general sat staring at Eli. Except for the flag in the corner the office was spare. There was one compact black computer terminal and no papers on his redwood desk. Who were the other partners? What was Eli's next question? No, backtrack, his last reply had been a misstep.

"Actually," Eli said, trying to pick up the general's rhythm, *"Newsweek* doesn't work me hard enough. It's not their fault; it's a problem throughout America. They've assigned me to do a soft essay on challenges facing Silicon Valley if peace breaks out. And I'll gladly give them their story. But I'm not sure that this *is* the story. Can I speak with you off the record?"

"Proceed," the general said.

"Well, I was wondering what's your vision for the future? You've got a reputation as a self-effacing, professional planner. How do you think the country could best use its high-tech resources?"

The telephone burped. The general excused himself, picked up the receiver, listened for a second and said, "Tell Marbles just to sit tight. I'll sign on in three minutes." Then he hung up. "I'm sorry. I doubt I can be of any help, but I'll think about your question. My secretary has a number where she can reach you."

Should Eli be insistent? On what could he insist? "Could I treat you to lunch some day this week?"

"I don't have lunch," the general said. "I work out."

"Great, I like to work out myself. Do you go for a midday jog?"

"No, I get my running out of the way before sunrise."

"So in the middle of the day, you . . ."

"I work out at the Ultra Club. All right, call my secretary in a couple of days. Maybe she can set something up."

"Great, I'd really appreciate that." Eli stood up to leave. On this spartan's spartan wall hung one tiny painting: a stick figure with a smiley face staring at an ignited match. Eli looked closer. It was a lovely painting. No, not lovely, penetrating. The stick figure's face was bluish white, haunting really. And the matchstick was scattering incandescent flames across the sky. The painting seemed out of the general's character—too whimsical and too arcane.

"Did you paint this?" Eli asked, reflexively camouflaging what he felt.

"Hardly. My wife inherited it from her father. When she hung it on that wall, she said, 'Good, now there's a little bit of culture in your valley.' "

"Your valley?"

"My wife likes to feel above business."

"I understand," Eli said. He could feel the general's growing impatience. Still, he picked the painting off the wall and turned it around. Gummed on the back was a fading typewritten caption: "When Evil explodes, the Good love Death. Paul Klee. 1940." And sure enough, when he turned it back around he saw Klee's little signature perfectly balancing the painting. The good stick man was

36

happily walking downward toward his death while the rocket consumed the sky.

"You'll have to leave now," the general said.

"Your wife has excellent taste."

On the drive back home, speeding along 280, then climbing out of "your valley," Eli thought: The general's wife must be the woman who'd called.

4

The Fastest Burner

Eli now dived headlong through his computer into the world of semiprivate information he'd discovered as a professional snoop. He hooked up with dozens of databases through *Newsweek*. About Redwood Partners he could find nothing. The firm wasn't incorporated in California or any other state; in Washington, D.C., it wasn't listed as eligible for Pentagon contracts. It hadn't paid any income taxes to California or Uncle Sam.

The accessible data on Maj. Gen. Wilson Powers, Jr. was more extensive. *Who's Who in the Military* indicated that he'd graduated first in his class at the Air Force Academy. He'd risen just as rapidly through the ranks; a passing mention in *Air Force* magazine dubbed him "the fastest burner." After a sabbatical at Stanford Business School, he'd become chief of operations at Vandenberg. Three years later, in the middle of the second Reagan administration, he'd resigned without comment.

There were no quotes from him in the mainstream press, ever. Asked by *Air Force* magazine what were his ambitions, he said simply: "To be a quiet patriot."

The news on his wife, Patricia, branched back to her father, Dr. Wilhelm Geist, who'd won the goddamn Nobel Prize for physics! His theoretical insights in the '30s had subsequently led to the invention of Nuclear Magnetic Resonance Imaging. A German Jew, he'd fled to Switzerland right before the war, then on to Stanford in the late '50s as a Distinguished Professor.

Patricia Powers herself had a B.A. from Berkeley, Phi Beta Kappa. Then a master of fine arts from Stanford. Prominent in California art circles, organizing this benefit, donating that painting — she seemed actively wealthy. Poking by way of credit rating services into her charge card records, Eli found that she spent thousands of dollars a month at I. Magnin's, Neiman's, Saks. She'd also donated, via her American Express, $10,000 each to Amnesty International and the Eisenhower Memorial Hospital in Rancho Mirage.

Shades of the celebrity beat. Eli knew what this second 10 grand meant: gratitude after drying out at the Betty Ford Clinic.

Using codes he'd obtained years ago from an accommodating administrator, he called up her Blue Cross file. This was amazingly easy to do — Eli had done it so often, he knew by heart the names of Elizabeth Taylor's and Michael Jackson's many doctors. He barely viewed such research as a transgression anymore.

Patricia Powers had indeed gone to the Betty

Ford Clinic for a month and had been a prime customer at Stanford University Hospital as well. She'd had five years of fertility work-ups. Diagnosis One: irregular ovulation. Prescription: Clomid. Diagnosis Two: husband's sperm count adequate, Mrs. Powers still the likely infertility candidate. Diagnosis Three: inhospitable cervical mucus that repels sperm. Then suddenly she incurred a flurry of charges on an emergency admission for a self-inflicted overdose. Was she blowing the whistle on her husband because she was one frustrated lady?

The general's private life was almost a relief. As far as Eli could discover, he spent next to nothing. His only credit card extravagance was twice-weekly $125 "luncheon specials" at the Fairmont. Didn't he claim never to have lunch?

His medical record was clean. Except for the sperm count ("profuse, with a tendency toward clumping"), he hadn't even had a physical within the past decade. His legal record listed one traffic misdemeanor. Eli checked out what proved to be a doozy: 130 miles an hour on 280 at night.

In a few days, Eli got a chance to ride with the speedy driver himself. He alternately flattered and wheedled Yuriko until she put him through again to the general. "Just one hour, sir. If you don't have any free time, we could work out together."

"You're hell-bent, aren't you, soldier?"

"Yes, sir. I'm afraid I am."

Eli pretended he was terrible with directions just so he could cadge some extra time on the drive over to the Ultra Club. The general met Eli in the

Sand Hill Road parking lot beside a mere Toyota with tinted windows. Once inside, Eli realized this wasn't an ordinary model. The polarized glass cast everything outside into sharp contrast. And the dashboard looked like the cockpit of a fighter jet. Eli asked about the various switches' the general turned on when starting the car.

"They're built-in detectors for radar, police radio and accelerating objects," the general said. Then added, "Not that you need these weapons in today's traffic."

Eli's seat automatically kneaded his back as the general wove through traffic. "You know I don't think we have these kind of Toyotas back East."

"It's a customized model," the general said. "Yuriko ordered it for me from Japan."

The general was visibly irritated by all the luxury cars clogging the fast lane midday on 101— Mercedeses, BMWs, Jaguars sniffing each other's tail pipes.

"How many Americans can afford the cars they're driving?" he asked rhetorically. "Damn few. This country whines about its deficit and still every mid-manager keeps banking on raises he may never see. There's no discipline anymore. No sacrifice. We're consuming ourselves silly while our rivals plot to dominate the future. Our kids' future."

He cut sharply across three lanes of traffic to exit near the Ultra Club. The club's interior was an unholy marriage of pink marble and power ferns. The general let Eli share his neatly kept locker.

As they were undressing, Eli tried to open up the discussion. "So, if you were in charge of Bush's Defense budget, what kinds of weapons would you advocate making?"

"Secret ones, of course."

Dressed only in black silk trunks, the muscular general led Eli to the workout room, whose floor, walls and ceiling were covered with mirrors. Eli's "The Whitney Houston Tour" T-shirt seemed inappropriate so he quietly slipped it off.

The moment Whitney Houston had become a crossover star, Eli now remembered, he'd heard rumors that she was gay. He proposed a story on "Sex Symbols After Rock Hudson." Could America still admire its Travoltas and the Travantis if it lost illusions about their sexuality? Wouldn't Lily Tomlin still be funny if the obvious about her were true? When Eli sent a series of queries out to the Los Angeles bureau, he got an uncharacteristically uncooperative reply that this story shouldn't fly. Why? Because Hollywood felt that it was no one's business.

Who is our bureau afraid of burning? Eli had wondered. Forbidden stories excited him the way that a nude covering her genitalia arouses attention. Eli would have persisted were he himself not conflicted about invading people's sexuality.

Why the hell was he thinking about this abortive story now?

He and Powers strapped themselves into adjacent Ultra exercise machines. Eli watched the general turn the dial to a precise muscle group and punch in duration. The German-built machine then swiveled like a contortionist and applied stress to the area selected.

There were perhaps 15 other lean, mean executives working out along with Powers and Eli. Evidently the social politics of this club dictated that one shouldn't look too closely at a fellow exerciser's distress. The grunting was low key, but intense.

"Simultaneous bowel movements," Eli grunted to himself in torment.

Whereas Eli was naturally strong, the general seemed unnaturally dedicated. He tortured his biceps, triceps, pecs, delts, lats, abductors, adductors, hamstrings, even his ankles for impossibly long stretches. No soft tissue was left on the animal.

"Try turning your setting to tensor fascia lata," Power told him.

Eli tried it and felt a crippling pressure on his knees.

"The whole man," Powers said. "Harden the whole man."

After his dad's heart attack, Eli had developed a phobia for medical knowledge. He couldn't remember, for example, whether rhomboids were in his back or his geometry lesson. Still, he got the point of the Ultra machine demonstration, which was to show that the general had no vulnerable sites.

Afterward, they relaxed in the Delphic room, which was also tiled with pink marble; a frieze

43

ribboning the walls showed nude men in triumphant poses. The naked general took a seat on the highest shelf, where the heat was profound. A small waterfall cascaded down onto hot rocks, emitting clouds of steam. Eli sat intimidated on a lower shelf. His time was almost up and he still hadn't asked a direct question.

"Are you wondering why I wanted to talk with you?" Eli asked. An amateur move. Once inside the door, a reporter never reminded his subject that a door existed.

"I assume that you would like to explore what I actually do." The general downed a cup of water, then looked down at Eli impassively. "Like most reporters, you probably started off with preconceptions. Now you want me to confirm your suspicions."

"Well, the truth is, sir, I was doing research at Stanford University Hospital on the health-care delivery systems in Silicon Valley, and I stumbled across data about your wife's attempted suicide." Eli couldn't believe his own ears. This was the crudest approach he'd made in years! He rationalized that he was following his intuition. Better first to probe areas of weakness. The time wasn't right to ask about weapons in space.

"It never ends," Powers muttered, then turned to see if anyone else in the Delphic room was listening.

An executive lying on the lowest shelf continued to stare up blankly through the mist.

"She's a goddamn black hole," Powers cursed through clenched teeth. "She's going to suck all of us in, one way or another."

5

The War of Elbows

"Soldier," the general said seconds later when he recovered control, "you're way out of line."

"Sir, I was only . . ."

General Powers gave Eli an icy glare that made the steam room suddenly uninhabitable.

"I'm sorry," Eli continued. "I apologize."

They quickly rinsed off in the shower room under high-pressure nozzles, then returned to the locker room to get dressed. In his last moment of nakedness the general said, "I don't know why in hell anyone attempts suicide. In my wife's case, she was under too much medical stress. She had the equivalent of a stress fracture. You've heard of metal fatigue—she had medical fatigue. But she's back in shape now."

"And another thing: how the hell did you see her medical records? That's a felonious invasion, isn't it?"

"Probably," Eli said, zipping up his pants. "The doctor who gave me all the records was just trying to help. He has a theory that there are more attempted suicides in Silicon Valley than anywhere else in the country."

"Bullshit. There are casualties everywhere. Casualties are a by-product of life."

They climbed into the general's car. On the ride back he drove even faster as he chewed Eli out. "When I discovered that you were an entertainment reporter, I couldn't put it together. Why would you be sticking your snout into my business? I guess I didn't understand that the press feels anybody's pain is a public affair."

"Maybe we should just talk about military affairs."

"Maybe we should just stop talking," the general said as he braked suddenly and swerved off the road. "Exit, insect."

Eli jogged a mile back to his car repeating, "Insect, insect." Then he drove home masticating the word. He was definitely out of line and probably out of his professional mind. Or else he was on to something. Hadn't Cher freaked out when Eli, before anyone else, had instinctively asked about her cosmetic surgeries?

When he pulled up to his cabin, the phone was ringing. He rushed frantically to pick up the receiver: it was his editor from New York.

"What on earth have you been doing? It's the middle of March. Or not to put too fine a point on it: Why the fuck aren't you back in the office?"

"I'm working on something big."

47

"Hey, who isn't? But the deal was you were supposed to take two months, max."

"I know, I'm sorry."

"Wonderful, you're sorry. Is that what they say in California now? Well, tell me, Mr. Sincere, what's this BIG story you're working on?"

"I think I've tapped into an underground military project in Silicon Valley. If I can assess its dimensions, I may be able to understand the motor driving this place, then . . ."

"Zzzzzzzzz."

He loathed his editor's mock-snore. Sparklin' Art, Eli called him, because he always asked for "more sparkle" in every story. "There's more—monstrous weapons in space."

"Since when did you become *Newsweek*'s military investigator?"

"Very funny. Well for once wouldn't it be nice if we had some teeth in one of our essays?"

"Essays aren't the place for teeth. If you turned up something, we'd have to turn it over to the boys at the front of the book."

"Yeah, and they'd sit on it until the story broke in the *Times*."

"Okay, you've got me a little interested. "What's this earth-shaking story?"

"I'm not going to tell you until I have it nailed down."

"And how long is that going to take? Not till the crappy weather is over in Manhattan, by any chance? Do you know that it's not even April and we're in the midst of brutal budget cuts already! I

48

can't believe it. Are you even working on that ridiculous *Weltanschauung* essay you pitched me?"

"It's 80 percent finished."

"Well, if you're not back in the office by Monday, April 3 with a 100 percent finished draft in hand, you're dead meat."

After the call, Eli found himself wishing that his editor would disappear. Such a vaporization was possible. In his decade at *Newsweek,* Eli had served under six editors. Most had moved upward on the food chain and disappeared into executive offices where they performed invisible tasks.

The previous one—his best—had taken early retirement. "To better position itself for today's more rigorous environment by restructuring," *Newsweek* had offered cash to practically anyone who would quit. Foremost among the seventy who split were those capable of getting better jobs elsewhere. Were only the lame left?

Eli put the National Magazine crown back on his head, stared into the mirror and gave himself the finger. The general's righteous rage had frightened him. From his basketball days he remembered that when you take a nasty elbow, you give a nastier elbow right back.

Newsweek had recently run an article on computer virus killers—the consultants hired to provide computer security. Eli signed onto the magazine and invaded the files of the reporter who'd gathered facts for the piece. After taking extensive notes, he located the number of a virus killer who consulted for the Defense Department.

He phoned the man and identified himself. *"Newsweek*'s thinking of doing a follow-up on the dangers facing the military's computers. Speaking off the record, what entryways worry you the most?"

"Not the obvious ones—that's for sure. We've protected direct access to classified data. It's the trap doors and the service entrances. The manholes that sloppy programmers leave unsealed in case they need to return for emergency repair work. I'm urging the Pentagon to protect these vulnerabilities."

Eli thanked the consultant.

The war of elbows sometimes escalated. Even in the Ivies, Eli kept encountering bodies tougher than his own. He accumulated injuries. The game stopped being fun. He—and then the varsity coach—felt Eli had no future in it. But his assorted injuries didn't stop hurting until Eli found another calling.

He now called Zack the Hack, an old friend who'd become a top analyst for Morgan Stanley. "Remember when I was at the *Voice*," he asked Zack, "how you helped me penetrate financial records by posing as a computer technician?"

"Times have changed, Eli."

"But don't takeover firms need to see a target company's real numbers?"

"That sort of thing can get you hauled off the Street in cuffs."

"I'm sure you're not doing anything illegal now. God knows, I wouldn't even contemplate it. But if

50

I promised you reviewer's tickets to any shows, might you lend me, just for old times' sake, some current service codes. And maybe some phone numbers and default passwords?"

Armed, Eli spent the next three days in his bedroom in front of his computer. Cautiously he worked his way from *Newsweek*'s technical services to a techs' hotline, where he scanned for a repair node on the Pentagon's payroll computer.

He pretended he was a specialist from IBM, then DEC, then Sun, then IBM again. As he remembered, these hotline hookups were quite forgiving to authorized servicemen. Sometimes he had to type a whole series of instructions on a blank screen without any prompting or feedback. But if he made a mistake, there was no penalty. Suddenly he walked through one entrance and found himself in the midst of the Pentagon's benefits data base.

He typed in the magic name: several Wilson Powerses flashed onto his screen. Sorting by rank, he found two Major General Powers, Jr. One was retired and drawing a pension, the other wasn't. Both had the same social security number.

The general must need an active status to access the Pentagon computer, Eli thought. Using his own phony super superuser status as a technician, Eli repeatedly asked the computer he was invading for "Help." Slowly he made his way from payroll onto the Pentagon's master financial database. Typing in the active Powers' identification numbers, he requested the general's current job assignment.

51

"USAF, Space Command."

Then he requested a list of financial directories to which Space Commander Powers had access. Only one directory — "BLHO" — came on the screen. This was easier than Eli expected.

Posing electronically as the general, he called up the BLHO file.

"WELCOME. YOU HAVE TEN SECONDS TO PASS CHECKS. PLEASE USE THE THUMB OF YOUR RIGHT HAND."

Jesus H. Christ!

Eli had heard about finger I.D. keys, but God knows he didn't have such a device on his small portable. A second later he realized that he didn't have the general's thumb.

When ten seconds had elapsed, another message appeared: "PLEASE WAIT FOR A SERVICE REPRESENTATIVE. SOMEONE WILL BE CALLING YOU SOON."

Eli tried to backtrack. Nothing happened. He tried "Control C." then "Control Alt Delete." Then "Control Break." Nothing! He was locked in place. Military security would be closing in imminently.

He could unplug his computer, but the hardwired lines might leave tracks back to his basket. He knew only one other emergency way to abort, which could crash the entire *Newsweek* system. It was eight-thirty on a Friday night, eleven-thirty New York time. On Friday, a closing day, many people were still working diligently on-screen in the office. He had no other choice. He split his screen, typed in the instructions that gave him system operator authority, then ordered an emergency systemwide shutdown. His screen went blank. He vowed not to sign on for several days.

Still, Eli thought, they might be able to trace the way I entered. And if the general ever gets word that someone from *Newsweek* tried to break into his directory, he'll really explode.

6

Patricia

Stymied and scared, Eli kept hoping for another phone call from General Powers' wife. None came. He drove down to Stanford's library to find out more about her and soon found himself driving in front of the Powers home. The general and Patricia, he discovered by electronically scanning the county records office, had inherited her parents' house in old Palo Alto. Title had passed directly from Dr. Geist to Patricia.

The house was a white clapboard with black shutters. Large enough to be a Victorian, the columns astride the doorway gave it the look of a restored colonial. Then again, the oddly slanted roof with dark glass tiles brought to mind a futuristic Dutch barn. Eli parked next door, in front of a rickety cottage whose front yard was overgrown with wildflowers.

The Powers front yard, dominated by an old live oak, was immaculately kept. Wisteria climbing trellises along the corners of the structure imparted gentility. They also prevented Eli from peeking in back.

He kept walking along the front sidewalk. The house on the far side looked like a Best Western motel. All foliage had been leveled to make way for a maximum stack of pink boxcars.

Continuing down the block, beneath a succession of tall palms and towering pines, Eli decided that Palo Alto couldn't decide whether it was the northern rim of Los Angeles or the southern rim of the Bay Area. He turned the corner into a deeper wealth of confusion. A bachelor's bungalow boasting two vintage Bentleys in its driveway sat next to a Hispanic mansion with three Volvos and formal Japanese gardens. Eli came full circle unable to catch an additional glimpse of the Powers home.

He climbed into his car and doubled back to Stanford's art department. A tasteful poster on a bulletin board indicated that Patricia Powers — her husband's name wasn't mentioned — was helping organize the benefit opening for San Jose's Technology and Art museum. He called the museum and wangled himself a press invitation.

On the night of the opening, as he was filling out his nametag at the reception desk, he asked if Mrs. Powers had arrived. "Yes, she's right over there. Should I introduce you?"

"No," Eli said. "I think we've already met."

She was surrounded by guests so at first he caught only golden glints. She was wearing a black evening gown whose arms were joined to the bodice by a gold webbing that stretched every time she made a gesture. And she made many. She was chatting, laughing, putting everyone at ease.

Her honey-colored hair was teased into loose curls. When she wasn't greeting a new arrival or gesturing to the band leader to perk up the tempo, she fussed with her hairdo. She seemed uncomfortable with it.

As soon as the crowd around her temporarily cleared, Eli approached: "Eli Franklin, *Newsweek*. Haven't we spoken before?"

"No," she said, lifting an eyebrow. "I don't believe so."

"I'm sure we've talked on the phone."

"That's very possible."

She was a striking woman. Generally Eli took little note of colors, but he noticed her green eyes and olive skin, which contrasted with her light hair and Nordic features.

"Did *Newsweek* send you out here to do a piece on our little museum?" she asked.

"Not really," he said. Her voice sounded exactly like the beckoning woman's on the phone! But apparently she didn't want to acknowledge their conversation here or now.

"I didn't imagine they would. Even the local paper has been dubious. Their reporters have been calling our International Technology and Art museum the T and A. Lovely. I suppose in this crass a valley such a nickname will attract patrons."

How self-destructive, Eli thought. Is she feeding all the reporters this kind of copy? He couldn't help gazing at her. A natural California beauty, she seemed pained by something. As they talked, she simultaneously looked away.

The mayor of San Jose came up to greet her. Eli stepped aside, got a drink, watched her charm her way through several conversations, tell one waiter to dim the lights slightly and another to freshen up the buffet table. Soon she brought a drink to the band leader and while he was sipping, she borrowed his baton and pretended to conduct a few measures. The band played along.

She was flamboyant *and* refined—just the sort of society woman Eli would normally have shied away from except in the line of duty. He was most comfortable dating colleagues—Nina, Susie—who could have been sisters. Patricia Powers projected class. Yet despite her facility in putting on a grand show, Eli sensed she lived elsewhere. Her face masked pain.

When the crowd around her thinned, he approached again and asked, "Could I trouble the queen of the castle for a quick tour?"

"My pleasure. Which wing would you like to look at first: The Art of Technology or the Technology of Art?"

Eli chose the art wing. Mrs. Powers led the way, casting caustic comments before them. She pointed to a ghostly female presence emerging from a dark red canvas. "That's one of Nathan Olivera's best, done in 1960. Then he got too much success, lost his magic and started imitating himself."

Reading the crystalline i.d., Eli noticed that the

painting was "A Pioneering Gift From the Patricia Powers Collection."

"Those labels are embarrassing," she said. "But no more embarrassing than the whole premise of the museum. If you rent an audio tour, you can hear Nate talking about how he achieved this hue and that impasto. Tell me: Is there *anything* more deadly than artists reducing creation to craft?"

"How about civilians creating monstrous weapons?"

"Sounds like you're working on something important," Mrs. Powers said dismissively, leading him into the technology wing.

Eli scolded himself: Don't be so crude. She doesn't want to talk about it now. Have you lost all professional cool!

They strolled quietly through three-dimensional models of microchips whose gates opened automatically when a human approached. Eli felt as if they were floating through a futuristic city. "More money went into this wing, didn't it?" he asked.

"Of course. Form follows funding."

Eli and Mrs. Powers were sauntering along when they almost entered a room where a bearded man was conversing with General Powers.

"He's here!" Eli whispered, tugging her back into the gallery.

"You know Dr. Forst?" she asked with wicked charm.

"Dr. Forst?"

"The man talking to my husband, the one wearing the Grateful Dead sweatshirt. An aging whiz kid isn't a pretty sight so I don't think that we should go back to stare, do you?"

"No," Eli said. Why had she taken him near the general in the first place? This woman *was* suicidal.

"You should listen to Forst on the guided tour tape. He works for my husband, but he talks as if he were at the forefront of the Renaissance. Apprenticing in computer 'architecture,' laboring to simplify disk drive 'aesthetics,' then peering into nature to master futuristic 'design.' At one point Dr. Forst actually compared himself to da Vinci!"

"What does he do for your husband?" Eli asked as he steered Patricia Powers back into the relative safety of the fine arts wing.

"Even if I knew, I wouldn't care. Anyway, I shouldn't be taking up so much of your time. I'd best get back to the reception area."

Again Eli found himself staring at her. As if her manner and conversation weren't enigmatic enough, she looked half-Mediterranean and half-Scandinavian. And seemed at war with herself.

"Is something wrong with my hair?" she asked.

"Not at all."

"I used to have it straightened, but I'm trying to loosen up. The curls are too much, aren't they?"

"Hardly."

"What art excites you?" she asked, trying to change the subject.

"Klee. I'm a big fan of Klee's."

"You are?"

"Well, I can't really warm up to him," Eli con-

59

tinued, "but his paintings are so penetrating they're impossible to ignore."

"Exactly my feelings. You'll have to come see our collection. My parents were friends of his."

"Impossible."

"Well, suit yourself."

"No, I'd love to come over. I meant: How could your parents actually know him?"

"They were neighbors for a while in Switzerland."

"Tell me more, you have to tell me everything."

"I can't now. We're being too conspicuous. Call me and we can set up a date."

7

Dangerous Liaison

Why did Eli want to get involved with General Powers' wife? Was she a stable source? Why did Eli really care about Powers or what secret project he was working on? But . . . why was Powers posing as a civilian? What kind of rogue weapon would require such a cover?

Eli thought about this while shopping at Fry's for a fingerprint key plus all the necessary doodads to hook it up. This supermarket of electronics *and* groceries was literally located off Midas Way in a suburban bunker that also housed Mirage Systems. Silicon Valley's pop surrealism defied credibility.

At the front of the store, racks of barbecue chips and computer chips stood opposite each other. Eli found a fingerprint I.D. key below a spring special: "Buy A Real Joystick For Your Flight Simulator." For $49.95, one could purchase a plastic replica of jet cockpit controls that activated computer combat games.

"Great buy," a salesman ventured. "We've also

got infrared goggles so that you can play in virtual night."

"I'm not into games," Eli said. "What I'm looking for—I'm sure you don't have it. But maybe you know where I might be able to purchase a fingerprinting kit."

"Right up in the sundries—next to the nail polishes."

Standing in the long checkout line, between flanks of snacks and Peanuts videos, behind executives stealing an hour from work not for a quickie but for a quicker microprocessor, Eli felt guilty about his purchases. He wondered: Is this how John Hinckley or Mark Chapman felt buying a weapon?

Seriously, why did he care about "BLHO," whatever it was? But what was it?

He decided to make one last attempt to approach the subject rationally. Professionally. The next morning he sat at his desk fully dressed, drank a mug of strong coffee and set up interviews with a couple of vice presidents at Silicon Valley firms holding major military contracts. The public relations chiefs sat in on both of his interviews. They needn't have worried. Nothing of substance, let alone importance, was said. No one had ever heard of "BLHO." Of course, if they had and it was a classified program like HALO or Milstar or Mentor or Ikon, they wouldn't be able to confirm or deny anything. But off the record and not for attribution, they frankly didn't have the slightest inkling what "BLHO" could be.

"If you find out," Lockheed's liaison with the Pentagon said, "let me know so can make a bid."

Meanwhile at night, when Eli should have been sleeping or at least writing his overdue essay, he lay in bed thinking about her, imagining her, imagining her imagining him. Was she defying him to persist?

The next morning Eli called Redwood Partners again and asked for the general. He planned to apologize and confess that he'd been skirting around one simple question: What is "BLHO"? If the general just admitted he was working in conjunction with the Air Force on a vital project that required security, Eli swore to himself he'd drop this whole inquiry. He could accept the need for state secrets. He wasn't a teenager, after all.

"I'm sorry," the receptionist said, "General Powers is in Texas on business. I don't expect him back this week."

She didn't even say that he'd be calling in for his messages, which he surely would. They both knew that whether or not the general was in town, Eli's calls would go unreturned.

After hanging up, Eli immediately dialed Patricia Powers. "I'm going to be down at Stanford doing research all this week and, if it's not an imposition, I'd like to accept your offer to look at your Klees."

"You're not imposing at all. Let's see: How about tomorrow afternoon at two?"

"Perfect."

She gave him directions, which he repeated, even though he already knew the way by heart.

The Powerses' white door was decorated with a bouquet of dried flowers that would have been perfect for a New England Thanksgiving. From the street, the structure had seemed substantial but not imposing. Once inside the front door, however, Eli realized that the house stretched back forever, spanning at least two lots.

She was wearing a loosely fitting, pale pink silk blouse and tight, charcoal gray pants, which he at first thought were suede. As she started showing him around, he realized they were supple glove leather.

Her house's interior was immaculately white. The dark glass roof was a sophisticated skylight that afforded the paintings on the walls — and there were dozens — natural illumination.

In the center of the house was a courtyard containing a full-size pool lined with midnight blue tiles.

"How can a retired military man afford all this?" he asked.

"It's not his house or his money," she said with casual contempt.

She gave him the full tour, framing with wit every item in her collection. She seemed painfully aware of every painting's ambitions and limitations.

She finally introduced her Klees by saying they were unknown except to insiders. Dr. Geist had willed them to her with the proviso that they stay in the family until the 21st century. "My father was convinced that Klee would eventually be recognized as an equal of Picasso's and that his paintings would be worth their weight in gold. Or diamonds, really, since most of his canvases are so teensy. I suppose that's the worst thing you can say about Klee: he's precious."

"But he delivers on his promise: he ignites the invisible world."

" 'Ignites?' You make him too courageous. He just illuminates the darkness for a moment."

"Don't you think illumination is a form of courage, especially if you're exposing evil?"

"Klee believed in evil. He just wanted to balance it with goodness," she said, leading him into the master bedroom. Facing the bed were matching Braques—abstract gray analyses without a trace of a face or music.

"What's that?" Eli asked, pointing to an almost luridly colored portrait hanging beside her walk-in closet.

"That's a Nuclear Magnetic Resonance image of someone's brain. My father leased his ideas to a bunch of medical technology companies. They're always sending me their latest pictures."

"Looking for the family seal of approval?"

"I suppose. Frankly, I haven't the faintest idea how NMR works. My father explained it to me dozens of times, but I immediately forgot. He'd get angry and I'd start giggling, even when I was in my twenties."

Do you miss your father, too, he wanted to ask,

but instead explained (he'd read this tidbit in a magazine) how superconductivity might soon make NMR machines cheap enough to have in every doctor's office.

"Oh, I know that just from the recent rush of royalty checks. It's just the physics part, or the magnetic part, or the nuclear part. Anyway, I've given up. I just think of them as post-modern X rays."

She made tea and crepes filled with homemade blood orange marmalade. He asked if she'd ever painted herself and when she tried to be dismissive, he persisted.

"In fact there is a Patricia Powers who paints tremendous horses," she said. "But my art seems to be painting myself into a corner."

"Why not just walk out?"

"Wouldn't it be nice if life were that simple?"

She clearly liked the unflinching attention Eli was visiting upon her. Had he not known she'd attempted suicide, he doubted he could have remained so relaxed and generous.

What a creepy thought! Was she damaged goods that he didn't have to worry about breaking? Or just the opposite: Because she'd touched bottom, could he discard his own tiresome airs? The illicit manner in which he learned about her medical history made his feelings all the more forbidden. He felt close to her in a way he couldn't articulate, let alone discuss.

But why on earth *would* a woman so alive try to kill herself? Why couldn't she just get a divorce? The expertly hidden circles of fatigue under her green eyes were the only signs of her distress. He felt terribly drawn to her.

"So why did you call me the other night?"

"Call you?" she said with a dark grin. "Are you sure you weren't dreaming?"

"I doubt it. I haven't been able to sleep much lately."

"Welcome to the club. I hardly ever get to sleep. I'm afraid I take after my mother in that regard."

"Was she an artist? Or a scientist like your father?" Eli asked. He often opened doors with modern women by not presuming that their mothers had been "mere" housewives.

"She was a betrayer."

"A what?"

"As far as I can see, a mother has two jobs: to protect her child and to provide access to the inner world. My mother ultimately failed on both counts."

On this note, Mrs. Powers rose and abruptly drew their first engagement to a close. Eli started to say, "I'm sorry . . ." She waved away his concern and any further conversation.

"Maybe we can talk more openly when we know each other better," she said, escorting him to the door.

"I'd like that."

Very early the next morning, at an hour bordering on unconscionable, he called her to report an item he'd just read in the *Times:* Klee's "Uplift and Away," a study of kitelike structures, had brought a record $5.2 million the previous night at Christie's in London.

"Given the time difference," she said, "that might have been right when we were talking."

"Just what I was thinking," Eli said, then continued paraphrasing from the article. "This price eclipsed the $3 million that had recently been paid for Klee's 'Nekropolis.' And catch this—this is why I called you so early—at the same auction, a Picasso went for a mere $7.4 million. So your father was right. Klee is gaining on him."

"One auction isn't sufficient evidence, is it?"

"You sound like an editor," Eli said, thinking a million other things. After they chatted some more, he reminded her that he'd be doing research at Stanford all week. "Might you have any free time when you could give me a tour of the campus's sculptures?"

"I'd love to, assuming you're up for seeing a lot of Rodin."

On their walk, the conversation flitted through centuries of art history. Eli had a hard time keeping up. He complimented her taste and reach, but chided her for a being a show-off. She laughed, then dashed ahead to discuss Thomas Hart Benton. A major Benton retrospective had just opened. "Surely *Newsweek* has reviewed it."

"To be honest," Eli said, conspiratorially, "I don't read our art reviews. I prefer *Time*'s critic."

"Well, if we're talking about American realism, I prefer," she mocked his whisper, "Edward Hopper.

68

Benton is so explicit and optimistic. Talk about American Vulgar."

Hopper. What Hopper paintings did Eli remember? Nighthawks at the diner, the Mobil gas station, the office at night where the old-fashioned boss is oblivious to the stare of his shapely secretary. What could Eli say that was trenchant? Or at least clever?

"I know what you mean about preferring the implicit and the gloomy. There's an early Hopper. A woman and a man are riding horses in Central Park. They're about to enter an underpass. Realistically nothing bad is going to happen, but you feel the ominous pregnancy of the moment. God, sometimes I loathe art talk!"

"I know what *you* mean. I also know the painting: The Bridle Path. But I think there's a third rider in the picture. And empty buildings in the background."

They returned to her empty house where she offered him, instead of a drink, a neatly rolled joint from a Tiffany cigarette case. He took only one puff. The thought of going to bed with her was enough of a high.

She took one deep drag to mark the end of an innocent dance.

The bedroom was equipped with blackout shades and insulation that shut out all ambient noise. Although Eli had done the courting, he felt swept off his feet. When the lights went out, she took the lead. Attempted suicide be damned, she came on in the dark like the stronger soul.

Her breasts were large, firm, perfectly shaped. She was secretly a bombshell. Her skin was as soft as he'd imagined, but she was surprisingly muscular. He gave into her. She set the rhythm. He was lost in her warmth and tempo, lost without any sense of weight or time. When they were finished, he found himself kissing her out of gratitude. For what?

She fell into a deep sleep. Slowly what passed for his senses returned. He tiptoed into the white-tiled bathroom to shower and get dressed. Obviously the general was still out of town, but why take chances. It was almost six P.M. Once dressed, he took out his fingerprinting kit. He sprayed the fine dust on the sink. Sure enough, a set of athletic-looking fingers magically appeared.

The general must do handstands while gargling, Eli thought. He needed this kind of sarcasm to justify what he was doing.

Patsy was still asleep when he left the bathroom, an imprint of the general's right thumb in his pocket. Should he deposit a note beside her? Too dangerous. He kissed her again before leaving.

8

Into the Black Hole

Armed with a cast made from the general's thumbprint and equipped with a finger key, Eli felt confident enough to reenter the Pentagon's system. He used the same back service entrance and climbed into payroll. What had taken him three days now took a few hours.

Hooked on the sheer joy of finding his electronic way, he didn't consider what he was doing. Some of the directions he'd learned by trial and error the first time around came so naturally that he mistook them for intuitions. Silicon Valley was intoxicating his brain.

He entered the Pentagon's master financial database and rearrived at the moment to sign on the BLHO directory. Fears flooded up. What if they'd put extra security as a result of his last misadventure? He fondled the general's clay thumb. What if they were waiting to apprehend him?

Screw it. Posing electronically as the general, he called up BLHO. The same "WELCOME. YOU HAVE TEN SECONDS TO PASS CHECKS. PLEASE USE THE THUMB OF YOUR RIGHT HAND" came on his screen.

Without pause he inserted the thumb into the key.

"PLEASE PRESS HARDER" came the response.

He did and "WELCOME TO THE BLACK HOLE DIRECTORY" came on his screen.

Of course! He'd known it all along. Why were the most obvious riddles the hardest ones to guess?

He pressed the Enter key and subdirectories labeled FY'81 up to FY'97 appeared.

Fiscal years. They'd been working on this project since the beginning of the Reagan administration, at least two years before the President had made his Star Wars speech. And they were planning to continue through other presidencies.

Eli called up FY'88.

"GRAND TOTAL: $2,600, budgeted and spent."

He scrolled down. Dozens of evocative but not quite English names appeared: "Cyrogenic Inductors"; "Lethality and Hardening"; "Test Beds."

He opened up "Test Beds" and a financial spreadsheet appeared that said "Page 1 of 13."

He puzzled over the figures, acronyms and equations crowding each page. "3600 Anti-Spoofing T-ology. 3400 = 45.72 3080 = 59.6"

How the hell was he supposed to figure these out? Many numbers were in decimals to the hundredth place, leading Eli to believe that 1.0 represented a million, and thus the grand total for the 1988 fiscal year was two billion six hundred million dollars.

He scrolled furiously through more numbers

until he came upon one lonely section of text: "Our financial responsibility includes all R&D, plus pretesting for the co-orbital anti-ASAT laser and the decoy brilliant pebble. DOE will absorb weapon production under clean-up. Space Command will handle all deployment costs for the prototype trinity under SuperPatriot research."

So the unnamed space weapon was traveling in a convoy with a protector and a decoy. No wonder they needed a huge Titan to launch this armada. As Eli congratulated himself for figuring this out, a message appeared on the top of his screen: "Will, I didn't expect you back so soon. How did the Pantex visit go? Is the White Express going to ship our Raindrop on time? (Marbles)"

Eli looked at his watch—5:30 in the morning. How did this Marbles know he'd signed on? And how should Eli respond?

Sign off immediately, he decided. But then he might not be able to enter the Black Hole again. Quickly, with a command period U, he called up the general's user profile to gather information for another break-in. He scanned the data quickly. "Authority Level 2." jumped out at him.

He split this screen and called up all names having this level authority.

"Marbles, Powers."

Who had more power? Eli called up "Authority Level 1."

"Marbles; Powers; Becker, Forst, Yee."

Ah, authority levels counted upward. Marbles is the boss. Since Eli was signed on as Powers, he had access to Forst's user profile. He called it up. Maybe he could break in next time as Dr. Forst.

"Forst: Architect, chief. Concepts group, vice chief. Systems integration, vice chief. T-ology, chief engineer."

As Eli was scanning this, another message appeared across the top of his screen: "I expect you to answer my questions promptly. Understand? Code Back Black (Marbles)"

For a millisecond, Eli contemplated sending this Marbles an innocuous message to buy time. "No time," he realized. This code must mean that Powers had to respond in a specific way instantaneously.

Eli ran out of the Black Hole to the master financial database, to benefits, to the hot line back to *Newsweek,* then back to his own computer basket as fast as he could.

He sat stunned at his terminal. What had he glimpsed? What had he learned? Because he'd pulled an all-nighter, his brain was working both much faster and much slower than normal. "Raindrop" hadn't shipped yet on "The White Express." Marbles was Powers' boss. Forst might be Eli's best avenue in.

When it was normal people's breakfast time, he called Patricia Powers. He didn't want her to think he'd abandoned her after a one-afternoon stand. She answered the phone with a lazy voice.

"Sounds like you just woke up," he said.

"I was lying here in bed thinking what a thief you are."

"Thief?" he asked, muffling his anxiety.

"Yes, you robbed me of my insomnia. I've been in bed for what seems like days, dreaming of tropical islands."

"Are you accusing me of being a soporific?"

"Exactly, a terrific soporific. When can I get some more?"

"Flattery will get you everywhere."

"Will it get me lunch?"

Eli felt as if he were being drawn in too quickly, losing control. "I'd love to, but I have to get some work done. I haven't gotten any work done since I met you."

"Work?" she laughed to herself, then added, "I suppose I have to pay for my sins as well. My husband's coming back in town this evening. I should be with him until *he* leaves for work again — probably ten minutes after he marches in the door."

"God," Eli said, "Is he really that blind?"

"Let's be generous and say he's got blinders on. He can't see *me* anymore."

"I call that blind, not to mention dumb."

"You can call Will any name you want. *I* do. But dumb is probably the least accurate. He can memorize hundreds of numbers, which I'm told makes him something of a genius. Anyway, how did we get onto my husband?"

"We were plotting when I could see you again? When would it be safe?"

"Nothing's ever safe. But let me look in our calendar." A minute later Patsy came back to the phone: "Well, he's got an overnight trip scheduled to something called JSTPS in Omaha next Tuesday. You could come over then."

Eli didn't completely trust her. Or himself, for that matter. He felt as if he'd already abused her trust. In the Powers' house, he'd go snooping for God knows what. "Tuesday's great. But let's get out of town. Let's go to the beach."

"Wonderful, I haven't been in a couple of years. I've been hopelessly landlocked."

Before they hung up, Eli tried but couldn't restrain himself. "As long as you have your address book in hand, could you give me Dr. Forst's phone number? I might interview him for a laugh."

Without hesitation or comment, Patsy gave him what he needed.

9

Forbidden Territory

"Dr. Forst," Eli said, *"Newsweek* sent me out to California to do a special article on the art of high tech. We're comparing our time to the Renaissance. I wonder if I could interview you over lunch."

"I suppose so," Forst said, "although I'm really quite busy."

"Where's a convenient spot for you?" Eli persisted, already hoping that a lunch might lead to a tour of Forst's workplace.

"Empirico's," Forst suggested.

A couple of days later Eli took the Fair Oaks exit from 101 into the middle of nowhere. He found himself driving amid trailer parks that had taken root as suburban subdivisions.

Dr. Forst's transplantation was equally unsettling.

Eli had discovered that Forst was one of the 32 who formed the Homebrew Computer Club on March 5, 1975 in a Menlo Park garage. Subsequent Silicon Valley chronicles called him a dedicated freethinker. At Homebrew's pioneering meetings, he berated "the computer priesthood that hides information from the public."

Forst suggested improvements in Intel's early microprocessor chips, even though he never worked for the company. He critiqued rudimentary disk drives. Then he created his own "Independence" computer and gave its design away freely. But soon after Apple's success, the Independence computer and Forst's name disappeared.

When Eli finally found his way to Empirico's, Forst was waiting. The glimpse Eli had caught in the museum was sufficient for recognition, though Forst's face was still obscured. He had unruly black hair and a full beard. Eli imagined Forst's head might look identical if it were upside down.

The hostess led them to a table three rooms back, past rows of men in white shirts with loosened ties. The restaurant itself was a sprawling subdivision. The uniformity of its occupants made Empirico's seem like the lone cafeteria in an enormous company town.

"Dr. Forst," Eli began effervescently, "I've been reading great things about your Independence computer. It was widely heralded, wasn't it?"

"Technologically, yes. But I got caught up in the hobbyist spirit of the times and failed to see into the nature of business. Its failure was mine."

"Hello, I'm Tina," a bleached blond woman introduced herself. "Can I bring you a drink?"

"Sure," Eli said, wanting to lubricate the lunch. "How about a wine from a great year — a 1975 Heitz Martha's Vineyard cabernet."

Dr. Forst nodded approvingly, then ordered a large plate of spaghetti. Eli followed suit, then asked, "So what are you working on now?"

"A little of this, a little of that. Puttering in my brain."

"Quite a brain, I'm told. I was over at the new museum the other day and saw your room."

"You mean my little corner."

"Well, that's just what I want to discuss. As I mentioned on the phone, I'm writing a *Newsweek* cover story on 'High Tech's Top Ten Artists.' "

"I'm not one of your top ten, am I?" Forst asked anxiously. "To the rest of the world, that would be laughable."

"The new *Newsweek* mocks conventional wisdom. Have you see our little 'CW' box up front?"

"I don't have time for light reading."

"It's no big deal," Eli said, downing his wine without regard for its vintage. "Anyway, my assignment is to find true dreamers—those trying to penetrate the nature of knowledge."

"Precisely the problem I've been working on my entire career."

If this was Forst's problem, why was he mucking in a black hole with the likes of Powers? "How are you attacking it?" Eli asked shamelessly.

"By turning the problem on its head. Everyone craves miniaturization—more power in less space. . . ."

Compact brains that can be launched easily, Eli thought.

". . . My system uses its *own* intelligence to keep conquering this frontier."

"Fascinating. What might be some applications?"

"They're limitless. That's the appeal."

"Well, could you give me a couple of hypothetical examples—say, one commercial and one military?"

"I can't say yet," Forst mumbled. The word "military" had evidently tripped a security wire in Forst's brain. He turned his full attention toward his plate of spaghetti. He was a sloppy eater.

While Eli ate, he searched for common political or aesthetic ground. In some fundamental ways, he was a conservative. He believed that while individual humans might change, human nature didn't. He admired the founding fathers for engineering a system balanced by competing self-interests.

"On the museum's audio tour," Eli said, "I noticed you mentioned da Vinci. He's one of my favorites. I particularly love the balance between betrayal and revelation in his Last Supper. It's a perfectly designed painting, don't you think?"

"I don't know anything about his art. I'm just interested in his studies of machines and chaos."

"Oh. Are you trying to harness chaos?"

"Yes and no. Actually I . . ." Forst looked at his watch. "I'd better go. We shouldn't be wasting any more of each other's time. Right now I really can't say anything the public would appreciate."

"I can appreciate that," Eli echoed and motioned for the waitress to bring their check. When

Tina came, Forst said out of nowhere, "You know you're very attractive. Could you give me your home phone number?"

"That's a nice offer, but my therapist told me to stop looking for love at work."

Dr. Forst shrugged off this setback as if he'd made a faulty keystroke on his computer. Then he told Eli, "I really must get back to my work."

"Thank you for your time," Eli said with a courteousness inversely proportional to his rage.

Eli left first. Walking briskly to his car, he muttered, "Light reading! Put down by a fucking emotional primitive!" When challenged, Eli believed that the First Amendment overruled the Fifth. Hostile sources had no right to withhold incriminating evidence.

Eli drove off—around the block. He'd followed publicity, paper and computer trails before, but never literally tailed anyone.

Forst pulled out of the parking lot in a bronze-colored BMW. He merged onto 101 and headed north. Eli stayed a few cars back. Forst pulled off immediately at the next exit. Had he noticed Eli?

This ramp took them past the Air Force's Blue Cube with its radar dishes staring into the sky. Eli followed cautiously through the maze of Lockheed buildings with only numbers to identify their complexes. Forst was heading back in the direction from which they'd come. Eli followed him onto an avenue named Java. Onto Bordeaux then off Cognac Court, the BMW drove through the parking lot of a dilapidated shopping strip, then

81

down a road that said "Not a Through Street."

At the end of this street was another sign: "Federal Superfund Site. Toxic Danger. Absolutely No Entrance."

Eli discreetly followed down this dirt road, which ended at a vacant industrial park—a handful of drab prefab buildings that had been tilted up but remained unoccupied. No cars were visible. Where had Forst's BMW gone?

A black BMW approached Eli from behind. Eli pulled to the side, peered into his mirror and pretended to be combing his hair. This BMW drove up to the freight entrance of what seemed like a vacant building. The driver held a card up to a rusted yellow fire hydrant. The driveway declined slightly and the BMW drove underground.

Eli turned back to the shopping strip. In the next few hours he observed several cars head down the dead end. Spying both invigorated and frustated Eli. Pumped up, he strained at the leash. When darkness came, he climbed out of his car and jogged to the industrial park's edge.

At six P.M., a luxury Jeep and a Volvo station wagon exited—probably family men heading home for dinner. Eli ran forward and hid behind bushes near the hydrant. No other departures for the next half hour, the next hour. Then the yuppie Jeep returned. When the man held his card up to the hydrant, Eli couldn't restrain himself. He slipped out and silently attached himself sideways to the rear of the car. He wrapped his feet around one oversized towing hook and held on tightly to the other.

As the Jeep drove down into a darkened chamber, Eli's torso barely scratched the ground.

The driver parked and exited. As soon as Eli heard an elevator door open and close, he dropped from his precarious perch at the back of the Jeep. He stared at his hands. They were white with fear and stained with grease. He held them up with admiration, then kissed them. He felt like an All Star again.

What next? Not the elevator, he thought. He'd be apprehended immediately. In a far corner of the garage was a grate. Without any regard for its weight—his arteries were pulsing with adrenaline— he lifted the grate out of the ground. The drop down looked to be eight feet. He took his chances: With a spinal jolt he landed on a steel floor.

Scouting along this floor, he came to another vertical tunnel, this one lined with a ladder. He stepped down twelve feet to a landing marked "5," then to the next marked "4." He climbed downward through levels separated by increasingly thick slabs of steel.

At "1," perhaps a hundred feet beneath the ground, he found himself in a maze of metallic corridors. Walking along cautiously, he noticed they were humming slightly. The farther he walked, the louder the humming became. He reversed directions, but the humming only intensified. He started to jog and a red light came on in the panels overhead, a light that followed him in whatever direction and at whatever velocity he moved.

He stopped and stood perfectly still. Had he gone too far? He was petrified in forbidden territory. The high-pitched hum transformed into a piercing alarm.

10

Breaching Security

As the alarm shrieked, two men wearing surgical gowns and masks closed in on Eli from opposite ends of the metallic corridor. "Identify yourself," said one.

"Immediately!" said the other.

Eli sprang to his own defense. He needed to make his own terror seem terrifying. "I'm from the Black Hole military security!" he shouted. *"Your* security is lax. Criminally lax. How was I able to penetrate this deeply? Your performances will be reviewed. Take me at once to Dr. Forst. We had lunch together today. Tell him Eli Franklin is back for a follow-up interview."

The men eyed each other while the red light above them continued to pulsate in unison with the shrieking alarm.

"All right," said one. "But first you'll have to pass through decontamination."

They snaked through the maze of corridors as the overhead light and alarm tracked Eli's progress. He pretended to be fuming. The other masked man said, "You know we're not with security. We're maintenance, just in charge of the purification units. We were just responding to a pollution alarm."

"Responsibility has to be shared at a facility this vital," Eli said officiously. Silently he ordered himself: Join ranks with your own righteousness!

"If you value your clearances, don't discuss this incident until it's been thoroughly analyzed," Eli added. "Not even with each other."

They continued their march in silence until they arrived at a wall that automatically parted.

"Here's our air shower."

"Fine," Eli said.

"You can just leave your dirty civvies on the floor."

Once inside the air shower, Eli tried to figure the damn thing out as quickly as possible. He took off his clothes and turned on all the nozzles. Cool, dry blasts of wind shoved him simultaneously in all directions, making him feel like a bombarded atom. He struggled to turn off the nozzles, then waited naked.

"Let's get moving!" he finally barked.

The opposite wall parted and the same maintenance men handed him a green gown and mask as well as transparent booties. This time they took an elevator up one flight to what was numbered the second floor.

A secretary sat in front of a curved metal door. "Dr. Forst is inside," she said.

Eli walked up to the door and it automatically parted. The dimly lit room beyond the threshold felt cavernous. When he stepped inside, the door shut behind him.

"Are you proud of yourself?" a voice emanated from the dark.

"Reasonably," Eli said. "After all, I haven't been professionally trained in this sort of thing."

"What sort of thing is this for you? A game?"

"I'm sure it's a lot more serious." Eli could barely discern the top half of Forst's figure.

"Serious for both of us. You've contaminated me. News of our contamination will spread."

"To General Powers?"

"Ah, so you were lying to me from the first."

"I wouldn't talk about lying."

"I've nothing to be ashamed of," Forst said. His upper torso was dimly visible.

"Is that so?" Eli continued, surprised that he was still on the offensive. "Directing a project to orbit weapons in space. Nothing shameful about that."

"I'm not directing the project, just certain parts of it. If I didn't do my job, someone else would. The only difference is they might not do it as well. Besides, with what authority do you question me?"

"With the authority of an ordinary citizen. If I'm not mistaken, we pay for your work."

"Spare me the classroom civics."

"If you'll spare me the just-a-German-citizen defense."

"I have *nothing* to defend!"

"All right," Eli continued, considering this an oblique invitation. "Then what's Raindrop?"

"Raindrop?"

"Now who's playing games. Tell me: What kind of weapon are you creating?"

"One that reduces the risk of nuclear holocaust."

"How?"

"By threatening to eliminate those who might conspire to attack."

"I'm not sure I follow you."

"You don't have to."

Eli surveyed the now visible figure in front of him—an aging hippie encased by a cylindrical desk. Eli asked, "When did you start working for the military?"

"When I stopped worrying about Vietnam. Don't stare at me with such contempt. You're the one trapped in the past. Believe me, the military has learned its lesson about fighting unwinnable wars."

"So you enlisted out of admiration?"

"It's no secret that the Pentagon controls most of the country's research money. Da Vinci designed weapons. He accepted the Borgias' patronage. I have my own ideas that need to be capitalized."

"Like what?"

Forst hesitated, then pressed a button on his desk: The walls of his circular office lit up. The two men were alone in the center of a sensuround theater on whose screen was an orderly line of red, yellow, blue and black cubes.

Forst pushed another button: One cube joined the next, creating multicolored buildings that multiplied into skyscrapers, then miniature cities. The speed of the display kept increasing and the scale decreasing as the shapes took on a chaotic life of their own.

"Neat, isn't it? My t-chip will ultimately be capable of a trillion teraflops. Do you have any idea how fast that is?"

"Of course," Eli said. He hadn't the faintest idea.

"But I'm not just greedy for speed," Forst continued. "My microprocessors compete with each other. Right now they're handling simple programs. But when I upgrade the software, my system will analyze itself for errors. 'So what?' you might say."

"I wouldn't say that," Eli said, trying to sound knowledgeably impressed. Forst might as well have been speaking a foreign language.

"From a manufacturing standpoint, it's a godsend. A bug plaguing some obscure subsection can't destroy our entire investment."

"You and the government are investment partners?"

"Would you prefer it if the Pentagon hired backward scientists? An enlightened engineer on the inside can have input."

"To put an Independence computer in a warhead?"

"In heads of all sorts! Someday my new T-ology computer will be declassified. And then everyone will be able to think in an extra dimension. Do you understand now? Haven't you ever felt your own flatness?"

Although the technology eluded Eli, he understood the bargain Forst had struck. "What extra dimension are you seeking?"

"I don't know—I'm just driven to find out. Like your reporting, my computer research is neutral."

"If it's so neutral," Eli said, gesturing at the cinematic rainbow swirling around the room, "why are we talking in a secret government facility underground?"

"Why, indeed," Forst said, with a sigh. "I've already said too much—and I'm sure it's all been overheard. Now we're both in over our heads." He picked up a phone receiver on his desk and, without dialing, mumbled something into it.

"The guard will escort you out." Forst pressed another button: The doors to his office spread open, letting in a blinding white light.

"Maybe I should . . ."

"Go," Forst said. "Go now! I was on the verge of a crucial insight when you snuck in like a worm."

"Your boss Powers already made the mistake of calling me an insect."

"Powers may think he's my boss, but I work for Marbles. He understands my mission."

Eli made a mental note of this discord.

"Maybe I'm the worm," Forst continued. "That's how you've made me feel. Now get out before they force me to press trespass charges. Or worse."

The guard waiting outside the door led Eli down

a corridor several blocks long. The corridor was posted with Special Access Required signs and glass that looked like the inside of a one-way mirror. As they walked along briskly, Eli could see dozens of white-shirted engineers sitting in front of computers in their own cubicles. The computer screens were much larger than the ones Eli had seen elsewhere, but otherwise these T-ology workers seemed like ordinary engineers playing expensive video games. Their ordinariness was extraordinary. The men in the gray flannel suits had migrated west where they'd shed their jackets and exchanged their ties for security badges.

The guard led Eli to an old-fashioned freight elevator. Bundled on it were Eli's own clothes. They'd been quickly laundered. "Give me the gown, mask and booties," the guard said.

Eli complied. As soon as he was naked, the elevator started to rise. He slipped on his old outfit as the elevator ascended into the night. He came aboveground at the end of the string of stores he'd passed on the way in — next to a huge air-conditioning vent and a "Hair Forever" shop.

11

The Catch

Patsy Powers drove up honking the horn of her white Mercedes convertible a half hour earlier than planned. Eli came out of his cabin smiling, but thinking, "Hey, whose affair is this?"

After they kissed, she offered to drive to the ocean in her car.

"Sure," he said.

She hurtled down the narrow highway toward Santa Cruz. From his passenger's seat perspective, curves and cars loomed large before Patsy reacted to them. Between their seats was a black plastic cassette holder. He nervously flipped it open to discover not tapes, but a mini-apothecary of tiny yellow pills with heart-shaped holes in them. Birth control?

"What are these?" he asked.

The convertible top was down; she seemed not to hear him.

"What are these?" he shouted.

"That's my old Valium kit," she said, apologetically. "Just for emergencies."

"We're not going to have any emergencies."

She swerved to avoid a truck. The motion tilted the pillbox in Eli's hands and its contents flew backward onto the highway.

"I'm sorry," he said. "I didn't mean . . ."

"That's OK. I have more stored away at home."

Why did she have more at home? Hadn't she pledged abstinence at Betty Ford's?

Out of her glove box he pulled another cassette holder: Linda Ronstadt's "Heart Like a Wheel." He hadn't expected this either. Early Ronstadt seemed too hip for her class.

The freeway, like Santa Cruz itself, ended anarchically. You had to find your own way to the beach. They couldn't find a parking spot near the Boardwalk so they drifted south. When Ronstadt finished singing "You're No Good," Patsy rewound the tape and played the song again at a higher volume.

They reached a harbor and decided to have lunch at a restaurant next to its mouth.

"It's starting to warm up," the waitress said. "Would you like to sit outside?"

Relaxing in the late morning sunlight, Eli took in his co-conspirator. A natural beauty, Patsy seemed afraid of fraying. The apricot, cashmere V-neck sweater she was wearing had to cost hundreds of dollars.

"I've discovered quite a bit about your husband's profession," he said.

"Whatever you know is more than I do."

Again he wondered: Why this pretense of ignorance? Then he asked, "Just how much does he tell you about his work?"

"He tells me that he can't ever tell me *anything*. When I venture the most innocent question he responds in an obscenely patronizing manner: 'I'll never be at liberty to discuss that.' Can you imagine such language in my own house!"

"Grotesque."

"Exactly: grotesque. And it's not as if I really care. I spent the most boring years of my life living next to Vandenberg while he was in charge of the 'Peacekeeper' program. Do you know what "Peacekeepers' are?"

"MX missiles, I think."

"See, all you boys know that. Everyone near Vandenberg certainly did. But to utter the taboo letters was to risk the death penalty. Can you imagine wasting your life guarding such transparent secrets?"

"Maybe he was afraid that once this curtain was opened, more valuable secrets might be exposed."

"As if I ever really cared about his toy missiles! I was trying to stay in touch with his life. When we first met, we never had secrets. We went for endless runs telling each other everything. That's how we met and courted—jogging all around Stanford."

Her salad and his crab came. He cracked the claws and felt greedy scooping out the meat. She'd been generous with him; why couldn't he give her something precious back?

"You know," he said, "probably 90 percent of

the husbands in Silicon Valley are obsessed by their work."

"I suppose. I just never imagined I'd be rejected by my own husband. That's not at all what I pictured when I was growing up."

He reached out and covered her hand. "Are you sure he's rejecting you? Sometimes men just get consumed by their projects."

"Oh, no. He's rejecting me. I'm certain he's having an affair with someone, probably his secretary."

"Yur . . . How do you know?"

"I know. For one thing, he's lost interest in making love with me. He just goes through the athletic motions." She kept her gaze downward.

Eli squeezed Patsy's hand. "God, he's misguided."

When the check came, Eli suggested that they go for a stroll.

"Which way?" she asked.

"Let's keep heading south."

They walked as close to the water as they could. In his newspapers that morning, Eli had read that cold rain was continuing in New York City. All winter a drought had been feared, but now week after week the reservoirs drearily filled up.

The weather here was sunny, but wild. Winds churned the Pacific. When he was a kid, Eli's family had vacationed regularly in Atlantic City along shores that now seemed lakelike. At the time, though, when he leapt into the waves, he held his father's hand for dear life.

If he helped Patsy out, Eli thought, she might open up. "And your father: what did he think of Will? He must have been thrilled?"

"How did you know?" Patsy asked.

"It just came to me."

"Well, he was ecstatic. Never happier about any man I'd brought home." Patsy's face stiffened.

"What's wrong?"

"I just remembered the time my father and I drove together to the hospital. I was going for another fertility workup and they were treating him for cancer."

Instead of a condolence, something else came to Eli. "You must have been mad that he'd blessed such a . . . sterile union."

"I'd always trusted him. I was a good daughter," she said. And started crying.

He hugged her with a tenderness that said, "Go on, I'm listening."

"You have to understand how brilliant my father was. He could see *into* nature without losing himself. He encouraged me to marry Will. How come he couldn't see how bad a relationship this would become?"

"Even geniuses can't see the future."

"Couldn't he see what was dead in front of him? Did he want me to lose myself as well?"

"That's a tough one," Eli said, bewildered. They reached the edge of Capitola. Small streams of beachgoers were passing by. "Maybe when your father feared he was dying, he lost his faith."

96

"Well, he assimilated so fast, all he remembered was that his parents were Jewish."

"I meant his faith in creation. Something grander than the technological imperative."

"The what?"

"The technological imperative. An Air Force general with a Stanford MBA could seem like the man of the future."

"The kind of fellow likely to father lots of boys?"

"Perhaps."

"One of whom, unlike his daughter, might have big enough balls to win another Nobel Prize?"

"You said it."

"But you led me to say it," Patsy said with a laugh.

For a weekday, the Capitola beach was surprisingly crowded. Eli and Patsy didn't have towels or Frisbees.

"I've got a great idea for a game," Eli said. He ran across to a grocery store and returned with half a dozen eggs. "I'm a Nobel Prize-winning egg tosser. And I'm going to share with you, and *you alone,* my tricks. The first trick is overcoming fear of failure." He tossed an egg in the air, not quite knowing what he was going to do next. At the last moment he stepped underneath and the egg cracked on his skull.

A small, scattered cheer came up from the beach.

"You're a nut," she said.

"Now you try it," Eli said, scooping the egg's remains out of his red hair.

"I can't," she said.

He looked at her cashmere sweater and decided she was probably right. "All right, I'll let you halfway off the hook. Just take an egg and crush it in your hands."

"OK." She held it in her palms and squeezed from both sides. Nothing happened.

"You're applying pressure too evenly. The pressure is canceling itself out. Give the egg a good smack."

She pulled one palm back and clapped it brutally, joyously against the other. Yolk and white and shell exploded out through her fingers. She shook the goo down to the sand.

"Now you're an initiate," Eli said. "The rest is easy. Just cradle the egg when I toss it to you. Don't grab it, just cradle it in its own rhythm."

He tossed her an egg from five feet away.

"Perfect," he said. "Now both of us have to take two giant steps back."

They did and she tossed it to him for an easy catch. And back. And back again. And again and again until they were lofting eggs effortlessly along the edge of the Pacific. When they were beyond the range of an underhand toss, Eli impulsively launched his egg out into the ocean. Patsy followed suit with eggs four, five and six. Then they headed home.

"Let's jog," Patsy said.

"Okay." And they ran to her car at a quick clip.

White designer jeans notwithstanding, her breasts jostling, she easily sustained eight-minute miles.

Once in her car, they rushed back to his cabin in no time flat. "Should we take showers first?" she asked.

"Why?"

"My hair's a mess."

"Don't be crazy. You're a natural beauty," he said, pulling her sweater over her head.

In bed, they silently took turns caressing. Gradually each let the other touch more intimately. Every part of Patsy—her full breasts, her shapely back, her athletic thighs—felt more familiar than before. And yet the sum of her parts was more mysterious. Eli felt giddily drawn into her.

Soon he was moving in subtle rhythms. Patsy had taken the lead again. She was arousing and using him to an extent he'd never yet permitted. Ordinarily he loved turning women on. His orgasms were the culminations of his seductions, the planting of a flag after a deft climb.

She kept moving him into and out of his place. He trusted her. He felt secure in her. When they came, an otherworldly charge rushed from his penis down to his feet. Then it climbed his spine and suffused his entire body. He'd never felt so alive and beyond control.

Seamlessly their lovemaking passed into dreammaking. When the phone rang, Eli had no idea how long he'd been unconscious. Patsy was still sleeping soundly. He grabbed the receiver so as not to disturb her.

"Congratulations," the muffled female voice said.

"Who's this?" Eli asked in a terrified whisper.

"You know: I called before. I am your old friend."

"You can't be," he said, staring aghast at Patsy's peaceful body.

"I had to offer my congratulations. You now know more than any outsider. You have them worried. They've moved up their launch plans. But I also bring warning: General Powers wishes to terminate you."

12

Fire

"Terminate?"

"Yes," the voice said. "They can't figure out who is driving you."

Patsy stirred in his bed.

"Who *is* driving me?" Eli whispered desperately. "Who *are* you?"

"Knowing who I am will not help. You have to go public immediately to save your life. Publicize it in your magazine next week. Others may pick up your story. Perhaps the international press."

"It's not that simple. I don't have any proof yet. Nothing that will convince my editors."

"Eli?" Patsy was waking up.

"Call back," he told the other woman on the phone. "Call me back tomorrow night."

"Who was that?" Patsy asked as Eli hung up.

"Someone from work."

She looked at the clock. It was almost midnight. "They call you this late. It's three in New York."

"They call me whenever they damn well please," Eli said, kissing her on the neck, trying to distract her.

She accepted his kisses, then stretched out with a yawn. "I should go home. Will's coming back early tomorrow morning."

"I thought he was off in Omaha for a couple of days."

"Oh, he had to speed up his schedule."

"Why didn't you tell me?"

"Tell you what?"

"Nothing," he said backpedaling. "I just imagined that you'd spend the night."

Patsy got up and embraced him. Then she asked if she could have the bedroom to herself while she got dressed.

"Sure," Eli said.

In the living room, in a state of frenzied hyperalertness, he thought he heard her dial the phone. Pressing his ear to his own bedroom door, he heard Patsy whisper, "For a long drive to the ocean. . . . No, from the top of the mountains. There's a gas station up here. . . . Well, maybe it's a station you don't know about! . . . Don't interrogate me. . . . I refuse to play cloak and dagger. What I have to tell you is straightforward. . . . Listen, I haven't done anything illicit, and if I had, I wouldn't be the first in our family. . . . I want out, I want you out, a clean break. . . . Well, you just think about it while I drive home. . . . Hurl anything you want, idiot. . . . Slit your own throat. . . . Listen: I don't love you. I don't hate you. And I'm not afraid of you anymore. It turns out that it wasn't *you* I was afraid of all along. . . . I'll explain when I get home.

Now's not the time to talk." And she hung up.

In less than a minute she bounced out of his bedroom fully dressed. Should he confront her? "Patsy," he said.

"Yes?"

"Do you think we've gone off the deep end?"

"No, I don't think so. I feel more grounded than I have in years."

He walked her out to her car, where they embraced and kissed again. Then he watched her speed down the hill.

Sleep was out of the question. He lay in bed twisting every big fact and small detail over and over and over. Early the next morning he finally admitted it: he was in way over his head. He hadn't the faintest idea who his secret caller was. He'd invaded General Powers' work and wife on false premises. He'd uncovered a volatile plot that far exceeded his investigative abilities. His life was allegedly at risk. And as a kicker: he was kissing off his job.

At seven, he called New York. Someone else answered his editor's direct line.

"Where's Sparklin' Art?" Eli asked. Sarcasm was often the best way to reestablish contact at *Newsweek*.

"Among the dearly departed," the voice at the other end deadpanned.

"Fired?"

"To whom am I speaking?"

"Eli Franklin. Who's this?"

"Your new supervisor, Wellington Steno."

Jesus, Steno—an upper-class prig who'd been stuck just short of real power for the past twenty years. "They actually fired Art? Why?"

"He failed to deliver the goods. Our domestic ad linage fell six percent while our postage and paper costs rose. The editorial goods must be delivered more efficiently."

"That's brutal. Art worked his ass off for *ten years.*" Eli lingered on the last two words. Already he was at work undermining Steno's sense of security and hence authority.

"Your empathy is noteworthy. But as it happens, you were some of the goods Arthur failed to deliver. I haven't noticed your byline in our product for quite some time."

"Art told me you had a copy glut and a shortage of space. He assigned me two stories out here and told me there was no rush on either of them." Eli hoped the poor departed bastard would forgive this defacement of his reputation.

"There's your former editor's problem in a nutshell. He failed to grasp the strenuous conditions under which we all now labor. Or fail to labor. If a writer does not write, he will soon be written off. I trust my meaning is clear."

"Damn that poor bastard! Well, Steno, thanks for setting me straight. As it happens, I can come back quickly. I'll take a flight out of here tomorrow morning. I'll see you on the tenth floor in a couple of days."

Eli hung up strangely relieved. He'd turn over his notes on Raindrop to the boys at front of the book and let them continue digging. He'd call Patsy from Manhattan and explain that he'd been summoned back to headquarters. Then he'd call his trusty celebrity sources for a few "Newsmaker" nuggets and pound out a quick profile of the hottest new TV star, whoever that was. Within a month, he'd be back living his old charmed life.

Cowardly? Prudent? He'd sort it out in a few weeks. For the moment he just needed to return with the professional minimum: some evidence. He decided to drive back to Dr. Forst's T-ology plant and photograph a car with a traceable license plate driving underground.

Traffic was racing down 17 at a lunatic pace. Unlike Santa Cruz-bound drifters, drivers on their way into Silicon Valley tried to overwhelm gravity. Eli shot onto the highway with his accelerator jammed to the floor.

He sped past storage facilities, industrial parks, shopping centers and more storage facilities, worrying that he'd missed the exit. Then he noticed the Air Force's Blue Cube sitting quietly ahead. He exited to Java, traced his way along Bordeaux to Cognac Court, where he parked inconspicuously near the "Hair Forever" store. He had a telephoto on his Minolta. Nothing terribly detailed was necessary, he assured himself, just a few snapshots to point the way for other reporters. But no cars came by in the first hour.

He drove through the shopping strip and waited at the beginning of the dead-end road. Another hour and no cars. He drove past the "Toxic Danger" sign to the edge of the industrial park. He'd certainly catch someone coming out for lunch. Lunchtime came and went. Not a hint of activity. While he was waiting, he took snapshots of the ostensibly vacant buildings. It was getting late. He had to return home to pack. He didn't want to be caught in Silicon Valley's afternoon rush hour, which started well before four.

He decided to drive up to the fire hydrant, take one quick photo and be on his way. Then he noticed that the hydrant had been changed. This one was newly painted yellow with fresh soil at its base. The bastards had relocated the entrance right after his break-in!

Well screw it! He'd done his best. Let the boys at the front of *Newsweek* decide how to proceed. If they chickened out, he'd leak the information to some hungrier friends in the New York media. Let the country fend for itself. He'd be free from the whole affair.

He drove back up the mountain to his cabin and hurried inside to his bedroom. He felt in a frightful rush to leave. He excavated his big suitcase from the bowels of the closet. If the woman called tonight, he planned to tape her conversation. But he wanted to be packed first. Packed and ready to split.

He tossed his suitcase onto the bed. Suddenly the mattress ignited as if it were a barbecue soaked with lighter fluid. He headed toward the door but his path was cut off by a curtain of flames.

He raised his right arm to shield himself from

106

the heat. Flames singed him. His arm was on fire. He was a dead man.

With his flaming arm in front of him as a battering ram, he launched himself full force at the picture window.

It cracked but didn't give. Again, with double his full force, he smashed into the glass.

He must have passed out on the other side because when he came to he was lying on the ground surrounded by sheets, blankets and firemen. His cabin was half-smouldering, half-aflame. He tried to get up to see the damage. They wouldn't let him.

"I'm all right," he said.

"Just lie there quietly and don't move."

He was freezing, he was burning. "It was arson. They tried to kill me. General Powers tried to murder me."

The firemen paid no attention. "An ambulance should be here in two minutes."

"Promise me you'll get the arson squad, the best detective," Eli pleaded. And then he passed out for good.

13

Framed

First he noticed the diaphanous curtain. Then the elevation of his head. Then his arms spread out to either side.

"Either . . . ether," he thought. His last time in a hospital, he'd inhaled ether. To have his tonsils out.

Now one arm was swathed in bandages. The other punctured with an I.V.

"Doctor!" he called. No one came.

Had he only thought about calling for a doctor? How long had he been in the hospital? His mind was swimming in a thermal pool. A doctor walked into the room. "A. Neal, M.D." said his plastic I.D. Over his bifocals, the doctor surveyed Eli.

"How am I, doc?"

"Lucky," Dr. Neal said. "Very lucky."

The doctor started to unwrap the dressing on Eli's right arm. The doctor's gentle touch triggered shock waves of pain. While swimming in his narcotized brain, Eli had forgotten how inflamed his flesh was.

"How bad am I?" Eli gasped.

"I'd have no way of knowing." The doctor chuckled. "Fairly bad, I imagine. But so are we all."

"I meant: 'How badly burned?' "

"Oh, not too bad. The worst is on your arm. I'll show you in a second, as soon as I remove the last layer. This will smart a bit."

The doctor delicately removed the final gauze, but he might as well have clawed off Eli's skin. The rawness was so scalding, Eli closed his eyes and dunked back into the warm narcotic pool. When he came up for light, his arm looked like scorched earth.

"Right here," Dr. Neal said, pointing to a crater on Eli's forearm, "I removed the dead skin and grafted in a patch from your thigh."

When had all this happened?

Eli looked at the hole in his arm. Although he'd been an Eagle Scout, he couldn't remember whether first- or third-degree burns were the worst. "Is that a third-degree burn?" he guessed.

"Nowadays we call it a 'full thickness' burn. This area around the graft, with all the blisters, we call that a 'partial thickness.' "

Dr. Neal peered objectively into the wound.

"In America," Eli asked, trying to bond with his healer, "how long does graft take to work?"

The doctor chuckled again. "If it doesn't take in forty-eight hours, we'll start over. But I'm optimistic."

Dr. Neal slathered white cream onto some

gauze, then started redressing Eli's arm. Again his touch was electrifying, electrocuting.

"Smarts, I imagine," the doctor said.

"Worst cases? How do they stand it?" Eli asked.

"Sometimes the worst cases don't feel as much pain because their nerve endings have been destroyed. All your skin's still alive—it's just on fire."

When Dr. Neal finished the rewrapping, Eli asked, "How long will I be in the hospital?"

"That depends on your insurance. Do you know the name of your carrier?"

"TakeBack . . . LifeCross . . . something like that."

"Sounds like an HMO. They'll probably diagnose you out of here in a day."

"My diagnosis depends on my health insurance?"

"That's not the way I'd want it either," the doctor said.

Ether. Eli remembered the hard rubber cone they'd held over his mouth. His father, who was assisting, told him to count backward starting at twenty. Eli wanted to show off for his father and make it all the way. But the ether overwhelmed him before he reached fifteen.

"Do you have someone nearby who can take care of you?"

"My brother Fred."

"Then you're better off getting out of here. Unlike our new residents, your brother won't experi-

110

ment with you. Sometimes the less we do, the better." Dr. Neal checked the I.V. in Eli's other arm. "I'll set you up with a portable painkiller. You'll cool down, bit by bit, on your own."

With that prognosis, the doctor started to leave.

Eli didn't want the doctor to leave. He asked, "Have they called a detective?"

"Oh, he's sitting right outside, trying to entertain my nurses. Be careful—I imagine he's shrewder than he looks."

Eli instinctively braced himself, which sent shivers up and down his inflamed body. A shout came out and a nurse came in. She asked for his brother's phone number, then if he'd like another shot of morphine.

"Definitely," Eli said.

He closed his eyes during the injection. When he opened them again, another man was standing beside him.

"Inspector Kemmix," the man said. "But you can call me Al."

"Are you my bodyguard or my long lost pal?"

The inspector looked suspicious. He was wearing a blue leisure suit with no tie. He had an aquiline face.

Eli elaborated: "That's from an old song by Paul Simon. 'You can call me Al.' I talked with him once at a party. Paul Simon, not Al. He's very short."

"Your landlord told me you were a reporter from New York," the inspector said. "They must

111

have some pretty wild parties back there."

"Pretty anxious parties. Everybody's worried how big they are."

"Like Paul Simon?"

"No, he's big. But maybe he's worried, too."

The inspector craned his neck, then with a sudden twitch rightward straightened his strong shoulders in his jacket.

"Excuse my babbling: I'm a little gorked."

"Understood. Just a couple of easy questions: How long were you smoking before the accident happened?"

"Smoking?" Eli asked.

"Yes, smoking."

"Do you think that mattress burst into flames from an old-fashioned cigarette?"

"Call it 'toking' if you want."

"Toking? . . . You think . . . you don't really think I pulled a Pryor?"

"You have any previous incidents?"

"I meant a Richard Pryor."

"Oh, the comic," the inspector said with relief. "Yeah, the same accident happened to him."

"No accident happened to me!' Eli said, incredulous. "They tried to murder me!"

"No kidding. Well, we found remnants of crack paraphernalia in the ashes of your bedroom."

Eli winced. If he had gone up in flames—in slow motion he saw himself instead of the suitcase land on the bed—his life would have been dismissed as a drug overdose. When Eli unwinced,

112

Inspector Kemmix was staring down at him.

"Let's cooperate," the inspector said. "I'll help you find these bad guys. Who sold you the crack?"

"You don't understand."

"Then help me."

"I don't think I can," Eli said.

"You'd better," the inspector threatened. "It'll go a lot smoother that way."

"Aren't you supposed to read me my rights?"

"I did, as soon as I walked in."

"When I was unconscious?"

The inspector snapped all the wrinkles out of his jacket. "You know I'm not a smart fellow like you. I just know one dumb thing: Them that starts the fires either gets burned or hangs around to look."

"Which one am I?"

"Both—I suspect."

Eli tried to stare directly back at the inspector. Staring augmented Eli's anguish. The morphine and the accusations were simultaneously peaking. "I can't talk anymore."

Eli closed his eyes and the inspector continued: "Let me advise you not to leave the scene of the crime unless, of course, you don't expect to live here anymore. If there's no chance that another one of your fires will flare up in my district, I don't see the point in pursuing this. A confession or a flight back east. You decide."

Eli saw stars a few feet from his eyes. A map of the universe tacked into the plaster of cottage cheese ceiling. Beside it was a poster of Magic Johnson driving to the hoop. A personally signed poster that he'd given to his 10-year-old nephew. Eli was lying on the top bunk of his nephew's bed.

He looked down and saw his brother and sister-in-law camped out on the floor reading the Sunday newspaper.

Faith noticed that Eli was awake. She nudged Fred.

"I'm sorry," Eli said softly.

"Sorry for what?" Fred asked, standing up.

"Sorry that I'm causing you trouble."

"Trouble? I'm the one who's sorry that my brother was in the hospital and I didn't even know about it."

Faith came over and stroked Eli's shivering head.

Fred said, "Faith wanted to put you in the lower bunk so you wouldn't fall out. But I know my little brother. You need to be in the open air, on the top, don't you?"

"You know your little brother," Eli said. He stiffened his lower jaw.

Fred came beside Eli, but didn't ask any questions. He rarely did. He was the faithful brother, not the inquisitive one. He accepted his life's frame. Living was difficult enough without asking the unanswerable.

"I'm so sorry." Eli started weeping. Whatever the cost and whomever he involved, Eli knew he would never turn back now. He reached out with his nonbandaged hand to touch his brother.

14

Intimations

The next few days, whenever Eli stopped concentrating on his wound and started contemplating his situation, the burn on his right arm set off shrieking alarms.

Dr. Neal had fitted Eli's other forearm with a Portable Patient Anesthetic Control device. The bulky strip of beige plastic reminded Eli of the antishoplifting tags that storeowners in Manhattan wired through the arms of their leather coats. Eli felt wired to his own hot skin.

He pressed the white button in the center of his PPAC. An electronic goat bleated back to reassure him that a microdose of Demerol was on its way. The newest medical theory went: Patients will dope themselves less if they can control their pain before it becomes a frightening opponent.

Eli lay back on the top bunk in his nephew's bedroom thinking about his opponent. General Powers had winged him. Was it a week ago? Eli saw himself flying through the window, then crashing to the ground. His house was on fire. He was a house on fire. He'd rolled around on the ground to smother the flames, saving himself by instinct. Or luck?

The Demerol calmed Eli enough so he could deduce that nothing fundamental had changed. If anything, Eli was more threatening to Powers now than before. If the general was a killer—and he'd certainly lived up to his reputation—why wouldn't he close in for the coup de grace?

Eli envisioned the general smothering him in bed. The general's sinewy hands pressed down on Eli's mouth and nose. Eli wrestled himself out of the bunk and landed on the floor.

Standing alone on semi-sensate legs, he decided to make his own fear seem frightening to his enemies. But the general thrived on threats. A hunch: Eli should make contact with Powers' superiors. And intimidate with intimations.

He walked slowly to the den—all his brother's family was either at work or school—and picked up the portable phone from its recharger. He first dialed information to get the Langley, Virginia area code. Then (703) 555-1212 and asked for the Central Intelligence Agency number.

"I have an employment office in Arlington and a main number in McLean. Which would you like?"

"Main."

"482-1100," said a neuter computer.

Eli dialed again. An operator answered with Southern breeze, "CIA."

"I'd like to speak with Mr. Marbles."

"Could you tell me what office he works in?"

"He's the head of the Black Hole Project."

"I don't have a listing for that name or department. May I ask who's calling?"

"Eli Franklin from *Newsweek*."

"Then let me connect you with our Public Affairs Office."

"No, thanks. I have a direct message for Mr Marbles. Tell him an article about the Black Hole, complete with budget figures, is going to appear on Monday in *Newsweek*. If he doesn't call me back today, these words are going to appear after his name: 'refused to comment.' "

"Sir, at what number can our Public Affairs Office reach you?"

"Mr. Marbles knows where I am," Eli said, then hung up.

And what if Marbles didn't work for the CIA? What if the Black Hole was supervised by USAF Space Command or the Defense Intelligence Agency or the NSA or the NRO or another agency whose acronym was unutterably classified? Well, hell, Eli thought, that's not my problem. Let the CIA earn its keep. They can track Marbles down.

And how might Powers' boss react to a publicity threat?

"Fuck it," Eli repeated to himself. "I'll find out who he is by how he responds."

As Eli breathed life back into his bravado, he reassured himself that his last tactic worked well enough with celebrities. A star's agency might put you off for weeks, but if you called with confirmation of admission to a rehabilitation clinic or detailed divorce dirt that you planned to print without comment, a sweet voice called Damage Control would ring back within an hour.

Sometimes, however, Damage Control would call your boss as well.

So Eli had to back up his own story. He dialed *Newsweek*.

"Good afternoon," Wellington Steno answered the phone.

"Wellington," Eli said, "this is Eli Franklin. Something terrible happened after we last spoke."

"I'm aware."

"You are?"

"Yes, an Inspector Kemmix inquired if you'd had any prior incidents with crack cocaine and if you were still employed by our company."

"Christ! Kemmix must be working for them. What did you tell him?"

"To the former I replied, 'Not to my knowledge.' And to the latter that he should check with my supervisors since I was no longer in charge of your case."

"My what?"

"Your case. That's what you've become—a case. I've recommended to the new assistant executive editor—Ms. Nina Perkin—that she remove you from the payroll."

"Nina?"

"Yes, one of your former paramours, I believe. But don't expect clemency. A weak decision in your favor would weaken her new managerial standing."

"I'm not looking for clemency."

"Frankly, I don't care what you're looking for."

"I've discovered a big story out here, Wellington. I need your professional cooperation. If someone from the CIA calls you . . ."

"The CIA? Aren't we getting in a bit over our head?"

"Listen to me: If they call, just confirm that I'm working on a story about space weapons."

"Mr Franklin, you have exited the known atmosphere and are drifting into realms I shudder to imagine. I shall not raise my voice in an effort to reach your distant ears. As of this conversation, I no longer consider your business my business until I am informed otherwise by Ms. Perkin."

He hung up.

Eli was marooned on the receiving end.

Nina. His old paramour? Nina Perkin was six years younger than Eli and quintessentially cute. Her stories had a suggestive edge that teased everyone and offended no one. She loved selling. "Marketing" and "journalism" were comfortable bedfellows in her mind. That's really why he'd broken up with her. Or was it simple jealousy? His sense that one day all-too-soon she'd climb two floors and be in a position to boss him.

Call Nina. But Patsy first. Make amends with the last woman he'd abandoned so he didn't feel like both victim *and* victimizer.

As he dialed, he prepared to hang up if the general picked up the phone. But he was greeted by her "Hello."

Her voice and a fear fleeted through him. Could she possibly have set the fire trap? Abetted her husband?

"Patsy, this is Eli."

"Where on earth have you been?" she asked with concerned indignation. "The phone company said your line was disconnected without a forwarding number. I thought you'd left without telling me."

"Listen, a lot has happened since that last phone call to your husband."

"What phone call?" Patsy asked, her tone switching to brassy anxiety.

"From my cabin. My former cabin."

"You heard me?"

"I couldn't help but . . ."

"God, I feel . . . so guilty. But I had to. You were my only way out. And I'm out now."

"Out?" Eli asked.

"We're getting divorced."

"He's agreed to that?"

121

"I don't need his agreement. I'm as free as you are."

Eli thought about his own state. "Hunted"—not "free"—was the first word that came to mind. "What has your husband said about me?"

"Your name has never come up. I'm sure he has suspicions that I've been seeing someone. But who you are is none of his business. Eli, can you imagine the pleasure I had telling him: 'I'm not at liberty to discuss who I may or may not be seeing!'"

Patsy emitted a delicious laugh, which Eli echoed nervously. Was she really on his side? Was he on hers?

"Patsy, I have a lot to tell you, too much to tell over the phone."

"Then come on over now."

"He's moved out already?"

"No. But he's working at a tracking station in Hawaii for the next couple of weeks."

"Hawaii?"

"That's what I said."

"Listen, we should meet somewhere else. Someplace less conflicated. I mean complicated. Where's a convenient spot for you downtown?"

"Well, I have a board meeting at the museum on Friday morning. The San Jose Fairmont's right there. We could meet in the entryway at, say, 1:30?"

"I'll see you then." He saw her exquisite face

122

and the little blond hairs on her arm. The next words emerged on their own: "I love you."

After hanging up, Eli wondered: Could I possibly be in love? Or am I a reckless conniver? Or both?

15

Bait

Marbles didn't call.

By Thursday morning, Eli suspected he'd over-played his hand. What cards was he holding? He looked down at one arm swathed in gauze and the other fitted with the anesthetic dispenser. He fiddled with the button on his PPAC and wondered if he should start another day with a little Demerol.

Why not? At first he was relieved when his brother's family went off to work and school, but now he felt simultaneously feverish and fatigued.

Escape one step at a time. Jog back into shape. His nephew's school with its track was a few miles away. He'd drive over. He went into his brother's drawers and fished out some running clothes. The fire had destroyed everything Eli had brought to the West Coast. His sole possession now was his rental car, which his brother had ferried down from the mountain. His brother had also lent him $300 cash while Eli waited for his new checks and credit cards to arrive.

At the door he wondered: What if Marbles calls

while I'm jogging? But Eli couldn't stand waiting any longer. He felt under house arrest.

His brother's house was on an eerily quiet cul-de-sac in Sunnyvale. Midmorning, there was no foot or lawn or street traffic, just dormant recreation vehicles. Every third house had a big boat camper or 4x4 or classic Porsche parked in its driveway. Eli climbed gingerly into his Mercury Sable. Just turning the key in the starter ignited the nerves in his right forearm. Using only his left arm to steer, he pulled out of the driveway. When he reached the corner, another engine started up. A small blue car emerged a few lengths back. At the next stop sign, he glanced into his rearview mirror. It was still there: a metallic blue Chevette with a large Asian man behind the wheel. Eli meandered around the neighborhood. The Chevette shadowed him for one block, then turned away.

Eli headed toward the freeway again, but soon noticed a brown car hanging half a block back. A root-beer-colored Ford Escort.

When he circled the block, the Escort split off. But then the metallic blue Chevette with its husky Asian driver reappeared.

"If they're tailing me," Eli's mind raced, "they're probably tapping my phone as well. So they heard me call *Newsweek* and heard Wellington Steno read me the riot act. No wonder Marbles called my bluff."

Eli headed back toward his brother's home. He

couldn't waste time jogging. His heart was already racing at a five-minute-mile pace.

When he made the final turn down the cul-de-sac, the Chevette slipped away.

Once inside, Eli looked at his PPAC with disgust. The last thing he needed was a cloudy brain. He ripped off the plastic strip. A little blood rose to the surface where the I.V. had been. He pressed his thumb on the puncture and considered his strategy.

He lacked overpowering force—he had to make them fear he was about to launch a surgical strike. This was the kind of threat that might bring them to the bargaining table. But only if they believed him. He had to supply clues that would recast his conversation with Steno.

He leafed through the yellow pages, then picked up the phone and dialed an 800 number.

"Federal Express, how may I help you?"

"I have a package for pickup," Eli said. "How quickly can a driver come by?"

"Usually within the hour, depending on your location. Do you have an account with us, sir?"

"I'm sending it collect to *Newsweek*." Then Eli supplied his brother's address.

After hanging up, Eli contemplated what kind of missive to send Nina. Code created credibility. Yes, he'd write to Nina as if she and he were the only ones in the know. Certainly Marbles and

Powers, of all people, would buy into a secret project that bypassed protocol.

The trouble was: Nina was the last one who'd really want to know. That's why he'd postponed calling her. She'd puncture him and his accusations with a few sharp questions. The last thing Eli wanted was to be dismissed by a former lover as a paranoid. He needed a message that would work on many levels. If he couldn't supply evidence, he could at least imply it.

Dear Nina,

The photos I've just developed show the sealed entrance to the underground Raindrop plant. Since I'm confident I can find the entrance they're using now (I've recovered enough to drive), I'll send you a complete set of prints by next week.

On this and other points, I'm working hard to make the truth believable.

Rest assured I'll be in touch soon with all the explanatory details you need.

I appreciate your trust in me and this special project.

Fondly, Eli

How else could he make her get the point? When he and Nina were lovers, they used to communicate by imaginary rock 'n' roll songs. He added a "P.S. I found a copy of Mythic Harvest's first hit—'Out on a Limb.' Remember how alive we felt dancing to it?"

He stared at this "P.S." then scissored it off in disgust. Too obvious. Too unprofessional. Too desperate.

The Federal Express van arrived within the hour. As Eli filled out the slip, he noticed "Your Billing Reference Information." With his left hand, he printed carefully in this space: "Re. Final Black Hole Details." That would goad Marbles to inspect the package!

When the van departed, Eli considered other lines of attack. His woman tipster. Who was she? The only name that came to mind was Yuriko Tanaka, Powers' secretary. She seemed an unlikely candidate. And yet her quiet manner made Eli suspicious.

He dialed Redwood Associates just to hear her voice again. "Hello. We're away from the office, but if you'd kindly leave your name and number, someone will get back to you shortly." There was a beep followed by silence. Eli listened to the silence. Had Yuriko accompanied Powers to Hawaii?

He hung up, then dialed and listened to the recording again. It didn't sound like the tipstress.

He hung up again and listened to his own silence. Eli believed that if he descended deeply enough into himself, he could dredge up impersonal truths. He hid this article of faith from others. It violated his profession's rules, though not his professional experience. His best scoops were hunches from the dark blue that he'd subsequently confirmed.

The door slammed and Eli levitated. It was his 10-year-old nephew, Aaron, home from school.

"Wanna shoot some hoops, Unc?"

"Not yet. Arm's not healed. And I'm waiting for a call."

"Excuses, excuses. You can play gin. Or chess."

Two hours later a distracted Eli had split four rounds of gin and was struggling to avoid checkmate when the phone rang. Eli jumped to get it.

"Mr. Franklin?"

"Yes."

"Frank Marbles. Sorry for the delay in returning your call. In the future, I'd prefer you not leave such a blunt message with mere operators."

"Well," Eli said, surprised by his own rage, "you left a fucking blunt message yourself. I don't appreciate attempts on my life."

"Let's be precise. *I* didn't attempt anything."

"The hand isn't responsible for its trigger finger?"

"Solely for the sake of discussion, let me venture that supervisors don't always have control of their employees."

"I see: the trigger finger got out of hand. And how should the target feel?"

"Not completely innocent. If you poke into a man's job, then poke into his wife—a man has to

129

respond. Otherwise, the next thing he knows, you might start poking under the hood of his car."

"Hilarious," Eli said. "Let's . . ."

"This isn't the proper line for communication. Even assuming that you aren't taping our conversation, others may be."

"Others?"

"How do you think your muse got your name and number in the first place?"

"Who is she?" Eli asked involuntarily.

"You really don't know, do you? And on this bed of ignorance and naïveté, you're prepared to publish an exposé? With photos, no less!"

Marbles had nibbled on Eli's bait. He was outraged, but also hungry. "I'd prefer a more informed article," Eli said, fishing confidently in the dark. "Enlighten me a bit and you might find I'm surprisingly helpful."

"And why should I take that risk?"

"Because you're not America's only patriot."

16

Stunning Grief

Marbles proposed a luncheon meeting in two days at the Quoc Te, a Vietnamese restaurant.

With time to kill, Eli found himself wondering if Andy Lamkin couldn't help him. After all, for his newsletter Lamkin laboriously documented military contracts.

Why hadn't Andy ever returned his call? Even assuming that he and Inez had gotten a divorce, why hadn't Inez passed on Eli's message? Or at least given Eli the courtesy of a response? The fact that Eli himself hadn't returned Andy's last couple of phone calls made Eli all the more upset. Andy would be the last person in the world to hold a grudge.

Eli's Rolodex had been engulfed by the fire so he called information. A lone "I. Lamkin" was listed without an address.

When a woman answered the phone, Eli asked, "Is this Inez Lamkin?"

"Yes."

"I'm sorry to trouble you. This is Eli Franklin, your ex-husband's old roommate."

The voice on the other end started to cry. Eli had really stepped into it this time. He held the receiver at a distance as she kept wailing. Californians were so damn emotional. She wasn't the first person in the world to get a divorce.

"Could you, could you . . ." he tried to get a word in just so he could curtail this transaction.

"He's not my ex-." Other mumbled words came out of the receiver.

"I'm sorry, I didn't hear you."

"Andy's dead. Dead. Dead."

How? When? "I'm sorry. I shouldn't be having this talk with you over the phone. Could I come over to visit?"

"I'm packing now. And we're leaving tomorrow for good. We have to leave by noon."

"I can come over in the morning," Eli said.

"If you want." And she gave her address in Mountain View.

The next morning on the freeway he thought about picking up a condolence present. Flowers were inappropriate since she was in the midst of moving. How about something for her daughter?

He detoured to a TOYS R US, where he bought a Sesame Street Playhouse and grabbed an extra pack of characters just so the house wouldn't seem underpopulated.

Back on 101, he drove toward Mountain View past Forst's Fair Oaks turnoff. Eli was still ridiculously nervous about this visit. He passed Moffett Field with its blimp-sized hangar. Ancient aircraft were lined up at the end of the expansive runway. These WW II vintage planes looked as if they could barely fly. Surprising that such a valuable piece of land was so underutilized.

He slowed down slightly to crane his neck. Traffic whizzed by.

The Lamkins' street was close to the freeway. Mountain View, which to Eli implied a vista from the heights, was surrounded by more elevated towns. It also lacked the overhanging foliage that gave neighboring Palo Alto the look of an established community.

An old VW van that had been repainted mustard sat, half-packed and with its side door slid open, in the driveway of the Lamkin house. Eli parked. With the boxed Sesame Street house in his hands, he walked over to the van.

Inez came out of the house with some raincoats draped over her arm. She had a chestnut-colored face that would have seemed gorgeous were she not scowling.

Eli introduced himself, then said, "I brought something for your daughter."

"She's over there." Inez nodded in the direction of the backyard.

A little girl was strapped into a harness attached by a guy wire to the clothesline. Given that the backyard was fenced in, this seemed like overkill.

"I don't like doing that to her," Inez said, "but I'm the only one here. My sisters couldn't come up this time."

"I understand."

"How could you understand? No one here understands how alone and mixed-up and frightened I feel. That's why Dolorescita and I are moving back to Mexico."

Eli felt as if he were standing in the middle of an open wound.

"Go ahead," Inez said. "Give her the present."

When Eli unlatched the little gate to the backyard, Dolorescita ran as far away as the guy wire would permit. She had her mommy's coloring and her daddy's leanness.

Instead of pursuing her, Eli sat down on a little patch of brown grass and unpacked the house. After nestling Ernie in an armchair, Bert in bed and Big Bird in his nest, Eli said, "They're yours, little Dolores. I'm going to help your mommy now."

He found Inez in the living room, folding up the antennae of an old television. Eli offered to carry it to the van.

"It took me years to get Andy to buy a TV," she said without accepting or rejecting Eli's offer.

134

"He said he didn't want to contaminate our house, but he was also cheap."

Eli took the TV, then several other loads out to the van. Finally Inez said, "I hope I wasn't rude on the phone. I got your message awhile back. I've been meaning to return your call. I've been waiting to feel . . ." She paused for a very long time.

"Can I ask how Andy died?" Eli asked tentatively.

"In a car accident." Her tone was flat.

"I'm sorry. Was it . . ."

"Andy's fault. He almost killed our baby girl." She handed Eli a box piled high with light green sheets.

When he returned from the van, Inez was in the bedroom yanking Andy's dusty pants off of their hangers. As she piled them into an old box, she asked, "Can I ask *you* a question?"

"Sure, anything."

"Did you and Andy take drugs in college?"

"I did. Everyone did, except Andy. He certainly didn't take any when we were freshmen. After that, I can't say for certain because we drifted out of touch."

"You weren't the only one."

"What do you mean?"

"Sometimes you think you know someone. You go through your whole life thinking you know

135

someone and then it turns out that maybe you didn't."

Had Andy been smoking dope while driving? Or doing harder drugs?

"Unlikely," Eli said aloud.

"What is?"

"I was just thinking that with Andy, of all people, what you saw was what you got. He was sincere in an old-fashioned way. Almost to a fault."

Inez dropped her head into her pants-filled hands and sobbed again. Her whole body shook. Eli couldn't bear the sight or the sound.

He put his arm around her. And remembered the time he'd felt closest to Andy. "You know Andy was very brave."

As Inez's heaves subsided, Eli continued: "He used to tutor kids in Harlem. One week a couple of Columbia's tutors were mugged. The Citizenship Council recommended that, until the police figured out what was happening, the tutors should remain on campus. Andy would have none of this."

Inez was listening.

"I offered to go with him that week. He was tutoring three teenagers. We walked up to one hundred and twenty-fifth, then across town into the heart of Harlem. All my antennae were out. I don't mind telling you I was scared shitless — there'd been riots in Harlem not so long before.

136

But Andy just kept sauntering along. All of a sudden he turned the purest white. 'What is it?' I asked. He wouldn't say. He was as panicked as I'd ever seen him."

"What was it?"

"He'd forgotten one student's name."

Inez burst out laughing. "Andy was so terrible with names."

"And embarrassed"—Eli kept his arm around her—"because he didn't want these teenagers to think he didn't care about them. He thought the missing name started with a vowel so we just stood there on a street corner in Harlem as I tried to jog his memory. I kept slowly repeating 'A-E-I-O-U,' like the caterpillar in *Alice in Wonderland*. We were quite a sight."

Inez kept laughing as she handed Eli the box of trousers and belts to take out to the van. "Help yourself to any of Andy's clothes."

Since the fire had destroyed all of his belongings, Eli needed some clothes. But Andy's style ran to the Salvation Army, midsixties. After Eli put the box in the van, he fished out the one item that didn't seem hopelessly dated—a calfskin belt. Just for old times' sake, he tried it on. Even though Eli was as thin as he'd been in two decades, the leather didn't reach around his waist.

When he returned, Inez was in the kitchen. She pulled out a large silver tray from the bottom drawer. "Andy inherited this, but we never used it because he wasn't comfortable eating off of silver." Her scowl was returning.

"I've got to go soon," she said. "After this load, I'll lock up."

Eli went to the backyard to check on little Dolores. She'd turned the Sesame Street house upside down. Bert and Ernie were perched on the windows. Big Bird was trapped alone inside.

Inez unharnessed her daughter, converted the house into a carrying case and carted everything to the van. Before her mother could strap her into her seat, Dolorescita lurched forward and kissed Eli on the cheek.

"That's a nice surprise," he said.

As Inez started to pull off, Eli noticed the garage was still open. "Don't you want to lock it?"

"It doesn't matter. It's just full of Andy's files. I thought about donating them to a library, but nobody was interested in his work when he was alive. Why should anybody care now?"

Before Eli could lie, Inez continued, "The new owner plans to bulldoze the garage. Land around here has become too valuable for the likes of our old buildings. The buyer paid me in cash. Andy's office space ended up making more money than Andy ever did."

Inez backed out of the driveway without saying good-bye.

Eli jogged after her and spoke above the lawnmower putt-putt of the VW's engine. "I forgot to tell you how the story ended. After we figured out the kid's name, Andy relaxed. The teenagers were waiting anxiously for him. They *would* have been terribly disappointed if he hadn't shown up. His persistence modeled theirs. They were in high school, but barely literate. He tutored them without embarrassment. I guess I'm trying to say that he was a good man."

Inez squeezed his hand. That was the best she could offer. Then she drove away down the treeless block.

"Jesus," Eli said to himself. As if he needed this additional grief!

He wandered into Andy's office. It was filled with file boxes, the cardboard kind that you assemble yourself. Dozens of them were stacked in alphabetical piles.

Eli opened the top "A." Inside were bulging files for Acurex, Advanced Micro Devices, Aerodyne, Aerojet. He pulled out Aerojet's. The front portion, called "Phase 1 Contractors," was subdivided into "Sensors" and "Weapons," each of which was subdivided into "Space-Based" and "Ground-Based."

"Narcolepsy alert," Eli said to himself. Compared to computer paths, paper trails were as inviting as a drive across Nebraska.

He flipped to Aerojet's "Weapons" folders. Stuck on the front of the "Space-Based Interceptor" section was a large "Post-it" reminder filled with Andy's sweet handwriting. It said, "See Martin Marietta's and Rockwell's other Subcontractors: Acurex, Aerodyne, Calspan, Ford Aerospace, GE, Honeywell, Kaman Science, Litton, LTV, McDonnell Douglas, Mission Research, Photon Research, Rockwell International, Space Vector, Teledyne Brown."

The sub-sub-subsection was filled with dozens of technical articles clipped from defense industry newsletters and magazines. Andy was acting as the public's librarian. While modern governments routinely kept secret files on their citizens, Andy accumulated files on suspicious companies. He was an ethical accountant waiting not for a reckoning, but for a day of national remorse.

Inez was probably right: If Eli couldn't bear the thought of plowing through these files, who could? Andy's day would never come.

Inez's inexhaustible grief had exhausted Eli. He felt as if he'd been stunned by the aftershock of a bomb exploding unseen in space. An electromagnetic pulse had short-circuited his sympathetic nervous system.

He sat down at Andy's desk, which also looked as if it had come from the Salvation Army. The desk had been untouched for six months. The calendar on top was opened to December 1988; Andy could get by with a mere Month-At-A-Glance because he had so few appointments.

The last entry Eli saw listed was "Lunch — Institute for International Peace — Q.T."

Strange. Maybe Inez was also right about being deceived. Maybe Andy was hiding something. Eli had never known Andy to use slang like "on the Q.T."

17

Wired

The Quoc Te, a Vietnamese restaurant in a neon orange bunker, sat opposite San Jose State. Marbles had promised to arrive around noon; Eli was supposed to sit at a table, order and start eating lunch.

Twelve-ten. Eli was scheduled to meet Patsy at 1:30 at the Fairmont. Only after Marbles had hung up did Eli realize he'd scheduled two luncheons on the same day. James Bond makes a guest appearance on *I Love Lucy*. Luckily, when Eli had pulled out a map of downtown San Jose, he'd discovered the two restaurants were only a couple of blocks apart.

Eli sat facing wallpaper that was pretending to be a birch forest. In front of the forest was a Vietnamese cashier and in front of Eli was a menu featuring some 300 items, many of them misspelled. Marbles had said that this was the best Vietnamese restaurant in the world outside of Saigon — a hint of Marbles' history — but Eli couldn't find an appetite for, say, "gried frsh deer."

He ordered a vegetable firepot. It came and

Marbles didn't. Eli could feel each second elapsing. He looked around the restaurant. Who was watching him? Why had he sat facing the back wall instead of the street? He switched sides and cursed his naïveté.

A big Vietnamese fellow sat down in the now-vacant chair.

"I'm sorry," Eli said. "That seat is taken."

The fellow took off his sunglasses and smiled at Eli. He was dark, more Melanesian than Asian. It was the man in the blue Chevette.

"You're expecting Frank Marbles?"

"You're Marbles?" Eli asked.

The fellow roared and slapped the table. "Yes, I'm the old devil himself!" He kept slapping the table with a violence that exceeded his amusement.

"So where's Marbles?" Eli asked.

"Right here on the table." The man directed Eli's glance to the sunglasses. "Put them on."

Eli picked up the aviator-style sunglasses. They were a bit heavier than expected but otherwise apparently normal. A "Singapore" label was stamped on the inside. Was this a joke? Eli slipped them on.

"Testing One . . . Two . . . Three . . . Testing One . . . Two . . . Three."

"What. . . ?"

"Please hold," a voice came into Eli's skull.

"Who. . . ?"

The Melanesian man lifted a finger up to Eli's

lips. "You're shouting. Just whisper. Mr. Marbles will hear you."

"Marbles?" Eli whispered.

"At your service," Marbles' voice whispered back into Eli's brain. "I apologize for not being able to meet you in person just yet. But this line of communication is safe for the moment."

"How are you talking to me?"

"It's a wonderful device, isn't it? The tradecraft boys have really outdone themselves."

"Tradecraft?" Eli mumbled.

"What did you say?" Marbles asked.

"How can you hear me?" Eli whispered.

"Through a plain old transmitter. It's just the power-to-size ratio that's remarkable. The technology inside these glasses was developed in Silicon Valley, not far from where you're sitting."

Eli looked around. He was sitting alone. His tail had disappeared.

"Where are *you?*" he asked Marbles.

"Metropolitan Washington."

"So your voice is coming . . ."

"Via satellite. A secure band, although one can never be sure."

Eli surveyed the restaurant. The waiter evidently thought Eli was trying to catch his attention. He came over to the table and asked if Eli had finished his firepot.

"Yes, I'm all finished."

"Cafe?"

"No, just a check."

The waiter departed and Marbles said, "You don't have to leave."

"I'm not comfortable sitting in a restaurant mumbling to myself."

"Look around. You'll notice you're insignificant. Half the Quoc Te's customers are plotting to take back Vietnam. The other half are figuring out how to take over their cousin's business."

Eli scanned the room again. Many of the Vietnamese patrons did look as if they could be hatching plots. Still, Eli resisted Marbles' patronizing put-down. "This scene looks less insidious to me than lunch at the Four Seasons."

"I wasn't being racist, just realistic. It's a working principle."

The waiter brought a bill. Eli paid with a ten and whispered, "I'm nervous here. Can we go for a walk?"

"Certainly. But take along the eyeglass case Ratu left on your table."

Eli pocketed the case and exited. Once outside, the lenses of his sunglasses darkened in the bright sunlight. This gizmo was fitted with creature comforts. The invitation to relax spurred Eli forward.

"In our last conversation," Eli said, walking down San Fernando, "you alleged that I had a dark muse. Who is she?"

"Vera Ulyanova. A colonel in the KGB."

"Give me a break!"

"I understand your incredulity. Dreamers like yourself sometimes overlook the obvious."

"Why is that?"

"Because the obvious offends your sensibilities. You'd prefer a more complicated world which the intelligent would naturally dominate. You see: I *do* understand. I'm a dreamer myself."

"And what kind of weapon system have you and General Powers dreamed up?"

"Relentless, aren't you?"

"Well, I'm not easily eliminated."

"That episode again. Without disowning or accepting responsibility, let me say that General Powers' strategy for dealing with threats is more radical than my own. He believes that punishment precedes judgment. That's what makes him such a tremendous project manager. And that's why Colonel Ulyanova has targeted him. Incidentally, you're not the first person she's used."

"For example?"

"She called an IRS auditor and pretended she was an employee who knew that Powers was cheating on his income taxes."

"You're kidding?"

"Hardly. This woman is a new breed of pest. A lapsed Marxist drunk on capitalist schemes. Even her own people resent her."

A car honked. Eli had strayed into a crosswalk. This corner had no curb. He took the sunglasses off to get his bearings. He was beside a Foto Mexico store advertising both wedding photos and funeral portraits.

He put the glasses back on. "Are you there?"

"We shouldn't talk much longer. Continuous signals attract attention."

"So, to get to the point: What exactly is Raindrop?"

"It's a research project, barely in the engineering phase. Any story you wrote would be wildly premature."

"Should the public wait 10 years until you're giving tours?"

"Sorry to disappoint you, but the public doesn't want tours."

"What do *you* think they want?"

"Reassurance that America has the nastiest, most advanced defense imaginable."

Although Eli was listening to a disembodied voice, he'd formed a mental picture. Frank Marbles brought to mind his old college professor, Lionel Trilling. World-weary eyes; patience so long as he detected intellectual progress. To enlist Marbles' patronage, Eli kept playing the misguided idealist.

"Well, what reassures me," he said, "is knowing the truth."

"That's why I'm encouraging you to meet with Colonel Ulyanova the next time she calls."

"What makes you think she'll call again?"

"She's hungry and we've whetted her appetite.

147

She believes you know where and when this so-called Raindrop might be tested."

"Where? When?"

"Please don't prod when I'm offering more than I need to. I'm taking a big risk with you. Once you see by whom you've been abused, I'm hoping you'll come to your senses. Remember, when she calls, just say you'll tell her everything you know if she meets you *in person*. I expect she'll arrange something."

"Then what?"

"Then put these glasses back on and call me. We'll need a sign-on voiceprint. I want you to say the word 'yes' now."

"Yes."

"Good. Repeat that a few times."

"Yes, yes, yes."

"Perfect. I'm turning our signal off now, but you can activate the transmitter any time by repeatedly saying 'yes.' Someone will always be monitoring. One last thing: keep these glasses in their case on your body at all times. And don't monkey with them. They're programmed to burn their own circuits if anyone pries inside."

18

Luncheon Special

One-forty. He was a little late for his second date, lunch with Patsy Powers. He followed the modern trolley tracks to the Fairmont, but she wasn't waiting underneath the gold awning. The day had become muggy, he noticed. San Jose endured summer heat equal to New York's, but without the relief of storms.

He went inside to the air conditioning — she wasn't there, either. The spare lobby was dominated by a surrealistic painting of two tremendous horses — a black departing and a white confronting. Eli waited beside the canvas until it dawned on him that this was the back entrance.

He rushed through the ground floor and saw Patsy outside the main entrance, pacing like a racehorse beneath the flags of America, California and San Jose.

"I'm sorry," he said, hurrying up to her. "I went to the wrong . . ."

"Never mind," she said, hugging him. "Let's just go eat. I'm famished."

She led the way in a light lavender dress, a cot-

149

ton weave more simply elegant than the restaurant they now entered. Les Saisons was trying hard. Evidently the maître d' knew Patsy because he greeted and seated them quickly in front of a re-frigerated, multi-tier wine rack. A ladder like one might find in a fine British library rolled along the outside providing access to the rack's upper reaches.

"You look stunning," Eli told her.

After he said this, he actually looked at Patsy. Her hair was less tinted and teased than when they'd first met. She seemed slightly fuller.

Patsy was looking directly back at him, gauging his reactions. At the T & A museum, she'd carried on her part of the conversation while glancing away. Now she rested her head in a half-clenched hand. Her green eyes scrutinized him more search-ingly than before. Or was he just seeing her from a different angle?

He picked up his water glass. It was empty. He felt inadequate before her earnest gaze. "Patsy, you know how you confessed that you were using me to get at your husband? Well, I was doing the same with you. Only worse."

"How so?"

"I've been investigating him."

"That doesn't surprise me." Her face puckered with injured pride.

When the waiter came over to leave menus, Patsy recoiled. As he walked away, she said, "That man's got terrible B.O., don't you think?"

Eli sniffed. "I don't smell anything. Anyway, in my defense, I thought you knew what I was doing. I thought you were seducing or—at the very least—cooperating with me."

"Why?"

"Well, it's complicated, but it turns out that another woman led me on."

"Great."

"What I mean is that some woman anonymously tipped me off about your husband and I thought she was you."

As the waiter filled their glasses, Patsy said aloud, "God, that smell is unbearable. How is one supposed to eat!"

"Please," Eli said reflexively.

"Don't 'please' me! If they want a first-class restaurant, they can't have their help running around unbathed." She stood up from the table and stormed out.

Eli sat silently for a moment. The waiter disappeared, leaving in his wake no smell Eli could detect. The small lunch crowd remained too quiet. Three men at a neighboring table silently sipped their drinks. After a few minutes, Eli left his high-back chair and went searching for Patsy.

The hotel vestibule, flanked by busts of classical goddesses, led upstairs to an Imperial Conference Room. No Patsy. Nor was she amid the palms of the sunken lobby. He peered outside the front entrance—a slap of hot air. He peeked into an open door humming with life—a vast nightclub being vacuumed by a team of maids. Scouring all around the hotel, he finally found her perched at a fancy soda fountain sipping a milkshake.

"I'm sorry," Eli said.

"Stop saying you're sorry. 'Sorrys' come too easily to you. It wasn't your fault. The waiter stunk and I was rude. I can be a terrible bitch."

Was she protecting herself by feigning toughness?

"Lately my nose has been like an animal's," she continued. "I'll go back afterward and make amends."

Eli looked around this soda fountain, which was more pleasant than Les Saisons. Amused cows stared out from paintings.

"Patsy, don't you want to hear . . ."

"What's the point in torturing us both? You don't have to explain what happened. You're under no obligation to see me again."

"It's precisely because I *want* to see you that I need to confess."

"Why?"

"Because I approached you with ulterior motives."

"You just milked me like any other source."

"True, but something else started happening." His eyes fixed on the small diamonds in her ears. He'd never gone out with anyone who wore diamond earrings, let alone at lunch. "You know if I hadn't been misled, I wouldn't have had the courage to approach you."

"Would you have wanted to?"

"I never would have admitted it."

"Tell me," Patsy said, edging back toward Eli, "what is it you wanted to find out about Will? Is he doing something wrong?"

"I think so."

"That doesn't surprise me."

"Why not?"

"Are we speaking on or off the record?"

The boyish waiter behind the counter asked Eli if he'd like anything. "The same as Mrs. Powers."

"Please, don't call me that," Patsy said as the waiter left. She placed her hand on top of Eli's. "I'm changing my name. Back to Geist."

"Maybe that's what we should be talking about." She was arousing him. He tried to shift attention away from himself. "How are you feeling?"

"Dizzy with freedom. And tired. For years I couldn't sleep. Now I go to bed early and get up late. But I'm finding my own rhythm and that's exhilarating!"

"Has he agreed to a divorce?"

"No. I'm sure he has lots of nasty tricks up his sleeves."

Eli envisioned the man's muscular arms and neatly folded sleeves.

"Will doesn't give up easily." Patsy continued.

153

"He doesn't give up, period. He's drawn to dominance the way other people are attracted to beauty. But I've already seen a lawyer who's told me not to worry. Since I inherited almost all our assets, they're not community property. My father and Will always kept me in the dark. It turns out I'm filthy rich!"

Eli's milkshake arrived. *Rich bitch,* he warned himself. She was too exciting. He removed his hand from hers, hoisted his glass by its old-fashioned metallic brace and clinked Patsy's: "Congratulations!"

She drank to that, then added, "And to think how bitterly Will used to complain about our taxes. One year we were audited and he acted as if the world had singled out him—its most dedicated public servant—for persecution."

Eli gulped. "How did the audit end?"

"Typically, Will never told me. One night I realized that he'd stopped complaining so I asked him. And he said, with that nasty little grin on his face, 'I've eliminated my auditor problem.' "

"Eliminated?"

"Everything for Will is a life-or-death battle."

The anxiety flooding Eli must have been transparent because Patsy asked, "What's wrong?"

Should he mention that her husband had tried to murder him? Or that he was on the verge of being fired? Or that his intrepid investigation might turn out to be fool's work as an unwitting

154

Soviet agent? "I shouldn't involve you in this story anymore. I've already contaminated our affair."

"That sounds wise," Patsy said. "Will always claimed that the 'need-to-know' guidelines protected everyone. Besides, I might not be the most sympathetic listener since I wish you weren't involved in anything but me."

Staring at this fair-haired, dark-skinned beauty dumbfounded Eli. She didn't like to mince words. She cut so easily to the heart of matters. Yet she also conspired to keep the drama going. Although she was inviting Eli into her dressing room, she didn't want to talk backstage.

Thinking about Patsy undressing caused Eli's pants to rise. He crossed his legs. Courting her felt riskier than seducing Marbles. What was the peril he still sensed around her?

Eli asked, "Shall I see if I can get us a room upstairs?"

Patsy nodded assent.

They strolled out of the fountain to the registration desk, where Eli asked for a room.

"I'm sorry, sir, but we're booked for the night."

"Well, as it happens," Eli continued, "my wife and I just have a few hours layover between flights. We'll be out of the room by five."

"I see—a layover," the clerk repeated without betraying a snicker. "In that case, I'm sure we can find something." He played with the computer while sneaking an approving glance at Patsy, who

155

was studying the Frank Stella drawings behind the counter.

"Monotonalism meeting monotony is no good," she concluded. "I prefer his wild emptiness."

As the clerk filled out a receipt, he said, "If you'd like, sir, I can list the charge as a 'luncheon special.' "

"It doesn't matter," Eli said while trying to remember where he'd seen that euphemism before. The general's American Express records!

Eli had gone out of his to meet Patsy on neutral turf. He didn't want to sleep in the general's bed anymore. If he was going to woo Patsy, he needed to believe it was in good faith. As he escorted a radiant Patsy onto the elevator, Eli wondered: Lust plus what? On whose behalf am I tracking this man?

Patsy touched his left arm. "You know when we first met at the museum I felt immediately connected to you. Dangerously connected. But I didn't know whether I was hungry for love or revenge."

19

The Real Thing

Laboring without apparent misconceptions, with nothing ostensibly to gain save each other, Eli made love to Patsy even more slowly than before. She was aroused by Eli's languorous kisses and responded with open-hearted sensuality. The moment he entered her again he felt entranced, as if a wondrously dark world had enveloped his eyes. He didn't need to see. All his other senses urged him toward senselessness.

Afterward, as she held him tight in her sleep, Eli wondered: Could she just be drawn to me because . . . just because she's drawn to me?

Then he worried: Why didn't she ask about the bandage on my arm? Is she bissfully oblivious? Or more aware than she lets on?

Someone knocked at the door. A woman asked, "Is your room ready for cleaning?"

Back at his brother's home, Eli's blank checks had arrived. The mail also contained an envelope from the Hyatt San Jose. This missive was post-marked July 3rd and forwarded from his address on Old Preacher's Road. Inside was a color brochure advertising the pleasures of a stay. A man was flirting while sipping wine in the Hyatt pool. But in order to fit into the envelope, the brochure and man had been scissored short.

Eli unfolded it. Inside the brochure were four strips of Scotch tape inscribed with phrases in blue ink. Since the brochure had a blue background with the same density, the writing was almost invisible. If Eli's mail was being X rayed, this message would have gone undetected.

Eli unpeeled the strips and affixed them on a sheet of white paper.

"Dear Brave Friend"

"Guadalupe off First"

"Five white posts reflect dead end"

"Share Diet Coke"

As Marbles had predicted, Eli's muse was coming forth.

Eli pulled out his AAA map. There were several Guadalupes, including a Guadalupe Parkway that ran on a parallel between the Guadalupe River and First Street. On his map they never intersected. Also, she'd omitted any mention of time. And if she'd sent this message to his old address, she probably didn't know about the fire. Was she an expert or an amateur? There were signs of both.

He decided to survey the area. Where directions

158

were concerned, he felt confident he could find his way.

Pulling out of his brother's driveway, he checked for a tail. None visible. He circled several blocks and noticed only more dormant recreation vehicles. For a dry valley, this place housed a ridiculous number of getaway boats. Instinctively Eli touched his shirt pocket to feel if the sunglasses were still there. Later he'd call Marbles.

He took the Bayshore to Guadalupe Parkway and drove down its length without encountering First Street. He cut over to First and drove back without encountering Guadalupe. When he passed the McDonnell Douglas and Watkins-Johnson buildings, he felt he'd gone too far. After another series of turns, he encountered FMC's property—a test track where they appeared to be racing tanks. Silicon Valley was the Pentagon's summer camp.

Eli crossed First again and found himself in yet another Orchard Industrial Park—a brand new office complex complete with flowing fountains. All the buildings were still vacant. The happy burbling of the fountains made Eli feel creepy, as if he were inspecting a new home built on spec whose hearth was blazing.

Pulling onto First again, he noticed a "Guadalupe" engraved into the newly poured curb. He looked behind him. Eureka! He could see five white wooden posts with reflectors on them. He'd almost missed this hidden dead end.

He made a U-turn and parked his car beside the last remnants of a real orchard. The trees were thick with leaves but no fruit. Their barrenness seemed an inkling of impending industrial blight.

No one was in the vicinity so he sidled up to the posts. Behind them was a makeshift dump dominated by McDonalds' litter. Amid the detritus was a half-buried Diet Coke can. Eli excavated it.

The top of the can had been partially serrated, then bent back into place. Eli wedged a small stick in the open edge next to "CA REDEMPTION" and pried back the lid. Inside was Hyatt notepaper.

"If you have gotten this far, I thank God you are alive.

We alone know what we are against.

We must now join puzzles.

Do you know where and when they will test Raindrop?"

Eli looked up. No one was apparently nearby. But the Red Lion Hotel was visible in the distance. The Hyatt was its neighbor. If Eli could see so many buildings, someone with binoculars could easily be monitoring him.

She'd thoughtfully supplied a tiny pencil and a second sheet of notepaper. He quickly scribbled a telegram of his own:

"Face to face we must join our puzzles.

Whoever you are, I must see you.

I know Raindrop's where and when."

He stuffed this note in the can, bent the lid back down and sauntered to his car.

On the drive home, he patted the sunglasses. Would Marbles really give him the information promised? If so, why? He decided not to alert Marbles until he played out this last gambit on his own.

A day later Eli returned. His note was gone. Nothing was left in reply.

The day after that, he returned and found in the can an airline ticket issued in his name. Lufthansa Flight 455—direct from San Francisco to Frankfurt. He was scheduled to leave in two days.

Taped onto the back of the ticket was a note:

"I am trusting your word. Please meet me for lunch in Frankfurt. I will find you at the arrival gate. We will both be on vacation from those who dread our free union. You are a brave man willing to go where others fear."

Eli slipped the note and ticket into his pocket, then hurled the can as far as he could into the barren orchard. Obviously both sides were eyeing Eli as a property ripe for development.

As soon as he returned to his brother's home, he put on the sunglasses. "Yes, yes, yes," he whispered.

No answer.

"Yes! Yes! Yes!" he shouted.

"Please stand by," came a neutral voice.

A minute later, Marbles: "Mr. Franklin, how can I help you?"

"She's sent me a ticket to Frankfurt, Germany."

"First-class work! I'm proud of you."

"So what should I do?"

"Meet her. See for yourself exactly who she is."

"She wants to know where and when you'll be test-firing. How did you inform her that I might have this information?"

"If she can work our system, we can work hers. Let's leave it at that."

"So where and when?"

"Late August or very early September."

"Back-to-School night?"

Marbles laughed. "It's just a test, mind you. Each side is testing all the time."

"And where?"

"In the South Pacific."

"As I remember, that's a fairly large ocean. Could you be a bit more specific?"

"Just tell her a test island within our South Pacific range. They have several 'Moma' class spy ships cruising nearby and dozens of military birds aloft. They can easily monitor the whole area."

Marbles' comradely tone disturbed Eli. Why would Marbles be feeding the Soviets information so profoundly hidden from the American public? The scenario was evolving quicker than Eli's scheming. "What do you want from Colonel Ulyanova?"

162

"For you to squeeze the most out of her while giving way the least information. Your business and mine aren't that different. When we compare notes soon, I'll show you exactly what I'm up to. You'll find I'm considerably more reflective than General Powers."

This last line teased Eli long after their conversation. Marbles' contempt for the general seemed genuine. Was Marbles contemptuous of everyone? Or was he offering Eli an elite channel of communication? While thinking about this and packing for his overnight in Germany, Eli realized that he didn't have a passport. His had expired in the flames.

He couldn't postpone his flight.

Well, if he could wear his brother's running shorts, he could borrow his passport for a couple of days. They looked enough alike. He went into his brother's desk and found the passport under "P" in a tattered accordion folder. Then he wrote an affectionate note explaining that he had to take a quick work trip abroad. He promised he'd bring back souvenirs.

This wasn't the first time Eli had left his brother suddenly. Fred had once accused Eli of trying to provoke heart attacks among all those who loved him.

Eli enjoyed the black humor he and his brother too rarely shared. Both had been young teenagers when they'd inherited the job of carrying their father's coffin. Who was left to blame for their murderous rage? Fred buried himself in a loving family; Eli fled to avoid sudden arrest.

Should he at least call Patsy? Give her his brother's phone number? No, the general might be monitoring her phone. Or she might tip the general off inadvertently. Or hurl some details as a weapon in their divorce battle.

Shouldn't he alert someone in case something happened to him? No, Patsy and his brother would urge him not to go. He glossed over all the dangers by guaranteeing Fred in a P.S. that this would be his last unexplained adventure.

Eli drove north to SFO and parked in the short-term garage. On his way to the gate, he paused in the international terminal's newsstand. All the world's newspapers and magazines were talking about China, the moral drama of the decade. Eli didn't buy anything. His solitary adventure was taking him in the opposite direction.

The Lufthansa flight left promptly at 2:45. A flight to Europe, he reassured himself, was no big deal. He'd done a reasonable amount of reporting in London. Once, when the exchange rate had been more favorable, he'd spent an extended weekend in Paris just shopping for suits.

After dinner, the shades were drawn and most of the passengers tried to sleep. The eleven-hour flight was scheduled to arrive at 10:30 A.M., German time. Eli closed his eyes and pictured Patsy sleeping beside him after they'd last made love. For all the women he'd slept with, he'd never studied anyone's rapid eye movements so closely before. Her body was soundly at rest as her eyes darted violently about—as if they were antiaircraft guns desperately shooting down incoming missiles. She was at war on another front. He longed for a peaceful time when they could share battle stories.

Since he couldn't sleep, Eli walked to the back of the plane to use the bathroom, get a cup of water and do a series of knee bends. His professional traveling regimen. When he returned, he found an envelope on his seat with a note inside:

"Are you prepared to face whole truth even if it goes against your preconceptions? Or confirms your suspicions? We are living in a new world without old borders. Please transfer flights without fears or fuss. Envious others may be watching us. Notice that you will be able to catch your flight back tomorrow from Frankfurt to San Francisco. You alone will be wiser."

Eli reached inside the envelope and found another ticket: Aeroflot to Moscow.

20

Maya

Who had delivered the note? Did "They may be watching us" mean that Colonel Ulyanova was herself aboard? The seat next to Eli was vacant. The nearest woman was tending two small children. As Eli ambled down the aisles, no one met his eyes. The middle of the night in the middle of the Atlantic. The Soviet Santa who'd slipped Eli the ticket didn't want recognition.

Eli returned to the airplane bathroom and put on Marbles' sunglasses. "Yes, yes, yes," he whispered. No return signal.

He pressed open the sink drain. As it noisily sucked air from the empty basin, Eli spit out, "Yes, yes, yes, yes." Again no response. Obviously this device wasn't equipped to handle airborne calls.

Once they landed in Frankfurt, Eli went to the Toilette. When the bathroom was momentarily empty, he burst out: "Yes! Yes! Yes! Yes!" No answer. Marbles had said the chances of a relay station establishing contact in Europe were iffy, but that Eli should take the glasses along and make repeated attempts.

An American G.I. entered. Eli slipped into a stall and waited. Soon another pair of infantry trousers shuffled in. These fellows loitered forever at the sink, probably combing their hair. Or else they were policing Eli. He flushed, then marched toward the Aeroflot gate along the high-tech corridor lined with duty-free shops.

The Aeroflot agents checked his ticket and directed him without comment to first class. Only one other passenger, a German businessman, was seated in this entire section. Once aloft, the two of them were feted with hors d'oeuvres—sardines, caviar, blini. Eli sauntered back to the curtain separating the cabins. The workers' paradise was crammed with hefty Russians holding on their laps even heftier shopping bags bulging with items purchased in the West. In the narrow aisle, one Aeroflot stewardess was distributing Saran-wrapped sandwiches while another poured apple juice from a jug.

Eli returned to his seat. Clouds obscured the landscape below. He dozed. In his dream dogs streamed onto the street as if freed from an enormous kennel. A borzoi hound insistently sniffed his crotch.

When the plane landed in Moscow, the stewardess stood guard at the first-class curtain. The rest of the passengers would wait until he and the Teutonic executive exited.

He walked into the terminal. Immediately he

was met by a tall, blond, fortyish woman who stared directly into his eyes. Hers were a light, almost clear, blue. "Eli Franklin?" The voice!

"Yes."

"You are a brave man. I salute your courage."

Instead of saluting, she embraced him, then resumed staring without embarrassment. She was sizing him up. She herself must have been six feet tall. She had a sleek face. Her hair—so light it seemed almost white—was brushed straight back over her head. She was wearing a brown business suit with a French scarf draped stylishly over one shoulder. She looked like Grace Kelly except her bearing, her internal gravity, suggested a character he couldn't remember from another film.

Eli asked, "What's your name?"

"My apologies for clumsiness. I am so excited at last to see you that I have forgotten common courtesy. I am Maya Gorkaya, at your service."

Maya Gorkaya? Not Vera Ulyanova? Could Marbles have obtained faulty information? Eli instinctively touched the sunglasses in the inside vest pocket of his herringbone jacket.

"Come," she said, "I have a car waiting."

She escorted Eli through the dim terminal whose copper-tubed ceiling glimmered with pre-industrial light. She had a businesslike walk. With a wave of her hand, she obtained free passage from the passport and customs guards. Either she'd prepared

168

them in advance or else she was so powerful they all knew her by sight.

When they approached a small black limo in a VIP area, two men popped out of the front seat. Both were wearing leather jackets with stylishly cut lapels. One opened the door for Eli, the other for Maya Gorkaya.

When everyone was inside and the car took off, Maya Gorkaya turned to Eli and asked, "Did you have pleasant flight?"

Her familiar tone disturbed him. He immediately tried to avoid his attraction to her. "I understand," he said, "that Intourist guides work for the KGB, but I didn't know it worked the other way around."

She raised one eyebrow and considered his remark. "You are a man who gets down to business. I admire that about you."

He wasn't going to swallow her flattery. Had she sized him up as someone desperate for praise?

"How did you obtain my name and phone number?" he asked.

"You have come a long way on faith," she said, her face quite near to his. "You have rights to know."

If he lost faith, Eli wondered, would he still have these rights?

"As you are certainly aware," she continued, "the United States government collects millions of Soviet phone calls each day by microwave inter-

169

cepts, then scans them for key data. Since we are not a rich country, we do not have the same capacities. We must pick and choose wisely. I picked General Powers' project. Then I listened. And listened. And when I overheard that you as well were curious about this project, I took the chance of using our communication relays to call you. Good connection, yes?"

"A KGB agent reaches out to touch someone."

"I have seen your television," she said, diverting his jab. "Far superior to ours."

"Tell me," Eli asked, "What have you found out about Powers' project?"

"My question to you, of course. But I will go first to establish trust. Are you ready for a bomb?" She seemed pleased with her control of colloquial English.

"I'm ready."

"Unfortunately it is no joke: He and his team want to orbit nuclear attack weapons."

"Nuclear attack weapons?"

"Missiles with nuclear warheads hovering over Moscow!" She lowered her tinted window and pointed out of the limo, which was now passing between rows of massive apartment buildings. "Such a system could fire down on us at a moment's notice and destroy the motherland's head."

"So Raindrop is an offshoot of Star Wars?"

"Not offshoot—it *is* Star Wars. From the beginning, Star Wars only makes sense as offensive system. The first strike before the rest of your missiles strike. This is why our leaders have begged your country to stop. Do you think the Soviet Union can tolerate such threat pointed at our brains? Of course not!" She gestured to the bright afternoon sky. "If disarmament fails, you will force us to orbit our own nuclear missiles above your cities. Then the heavens will be filled with monstrous weapons capable of destroying Earth in three minutes."

"Three minutes?" Eli winced.

"Or less. Is this the world we want our children to live in?"

As her rhetoric soared skyward, the celebrity reporter in Eli searched for a personal angle. "Do you have any children?"

"I am modern career woman, taking advantage of freedom while helping grow my country up. Do you have children?"

"Not that I know of."

The driver snorted like a schoolboy.

"Boys," Maya said, shaking her head. "Boys—the world over."

Their car was now in the thick of downtown Moscow at the end of a sweaty workday. Crowds of Muscovites were rushing about their business. Eli felt that he wasn't in a modern totalitarian state, but an early 20th-century city—say, Chicago. He asked, "Where are we heading?"

"I have booked you into the hotel with the best

character. Parts are undergoing renovation, but not my rooms. Then we will go to the moment's restaurant—the Cafe Perestroika."

They pulled up to the Metropole Hotel, which was encased by scaffolding. While her boys waited outside, Maya Gorkaya led Eli under the scaffold, then up an old marble staircase. "Lenin fought to capture this hotel. After he seized it, he gave speeches here. And after the Revolution became secure, it housed a state bureau."

She led Eli past construction rubble to an elevator. They rose to the top floor and walked to a corner door. She had a key in her pocket. State Security must have this room on long-term lease.

The room was two rooms—each the size of Bulgaria. Their enormousness was emphasized by opulent chandeliers and the spareness of the furniture. A desk here, an antique bureau there, a worn carpet, no TV.

"Fresh up. I will be waiting in the car outside."

Eli tested the mattress, sampled bruised fruit from a basket, noted the small box of detergent and extra tubes of toothpaste in the bathroom. Pathetic as these amenities were, Maya Gorkaya was trying to make him feel like an honored guest of the state.

Just to test the perimeter of his already too-guided tour, Eli took the steps downstairs. He exited at the mouth of a palatial, skylighted ballroom that looked as if it had been conceived at the turn of the century. Its walls were being stripped back, apparently in a search for the original design. In a far corner of the room several slot machines had been uncrated, perhaps for use in a tourist casino. The machine's back had been pried open. For checking? For rigging?

Eli continued out the front entrance. The limo had pulled completely up onto the already disrupted sidewalk forcing pedestrians into the street. The two guards were leaning defiantly against opposite doors, daring passersby to protest.

Maya was relaxing alone in the back seat. For all the world, she looked like Don Corleone.

21

Eli's Music

The Cafe Perestroika's front window was decorated with American Express, Visa and Eurocard stickers. Maya Gorkaya escorted Eli in and announced herself to the maître d'. The maître d' checked his list for the night, then shook his head, "No." They exchanged words. Eli couldn't understand the Russian words but knew they were unpleasant. When the maître d' showed Maya to the door, she swiveled back toward the dining room. He held her. She pushed him. A full-fledged shoving match ensued.

Eli had never seen anything like this in a restaurant. Maya Gorkaya was winning not because she was stronger—perhaps she was—but because she was utterly resolute. She harbored no doubts about her right to shove. She propelled the maître d' past his station into the midst of the well-heeled diners. He shrugged disgustedly and motioned to an empty table.

"Come," Maya gestured to Eli.

"What was *that* about?" Eli asked.

"Cooperatives! These new managers are more

corrupt than the old bureaucrats. Some day they'll find themselves on the wrong side of new laws."

"You had a reservation?" Eli asked.

"If I were man in my position, would I need one?" She pointed to a table in the corner where two bemedaled army officers were entertaining two heavily made-up women. "Do you think those whores had reservations?"

Maya stopped a waiter in a tuxedo and ordered drinks and "cutleti." He returned with two tall glasses and a pitcher of water.

"Officially alcohol isn't allowed in these new enterprises," Maya explained. She filled their glasses and proposed a toast. "To new friendship. To open exchange."

As Eli drank what turned out to be chilled vodka, he wondered whether she had begun their new friendship by lying about her name.

"You prefer sparkling California water?" she asked.

Was she referring to Patsy? Before Eli could decide, Maya continued, "So, in your note you indicated that you've discovered where and when Powers will stage his first success."

"You're certain he'll succeed?"

"Bulls' eyes can always be found. More care is lavished on the test target than the weapon. Once the generals report a successful test"—she gestured to the officers dining nearby—"no politician will risk refusing them. Certainly not a man so eager for winnable battles as your President Bush."

"So you suspect that Bush isn't clued in yet?"

"I suspect your President has preserved his . . . deniability. Is this an English word?"

"A sophisticated one."

Maya raised her glass in linguistic triumph and encouraged Eli to drink once more.

Their dinners arrived. The cutleti looked like large filet mignons. When Eli cut into the beef, it was incredibly tender. Then he took a bite: chopped, breaded meat that had been reshaped into a filet.

"So good as in America?" Maya asked.

Did *glasnost* extend to dinner pleasantries? "Almost."

"Ahh, you are such liar. These cutlets are ground up because our meat is tougher than Gorbachev's iron teeth."

She ate her cutlet heartily as the band, also dressed in tuxedos, played an impossibly schmaltzy version of "Born to Run."

"You have written about this rock poet of the masses?"

"How did you know?"

"We are not such a backward country. I read both *Newsweek* and *Time,* although delivery service is not what one would like."

Unfortunately Maya was flattering Eli with one of his own tricks. Research a newly famous starlet

176

to death, then pretend as if you've been a fan forever.

"Your study of Springsteen was very keen. I was
struck by your disappointment toward him. And
the black man Cosby. And the interrogator Wallace. And the conservative philosopher Wolfe.
False consciousness angers you, am I correct?"

"Yes," he said, cringing inside. He yearned for
such praise, but not from this dark quarter. "If I'd
investigated *you,* what would I have discovered?"

"Come. You will come to my office. To rest
your suspicions, I'll show you everything."

They finished their meal while the band played
Beatles' songs. The medley began at a Musak
pace, making "Strawberry Fields" seem intermina-
ble. Then an accelerated tempo transformed "Sgt.
Pepper's" songs into apocalyptic ditties. Striving to
grasp western music, the aging band seemed simultaneously desperate and self-mocking.

Maya Gorkaya rose. When the maître d' saw
that she was about to leave, he came over to offer
his apologies. Maya accepted his new obeisant attitude (he'd obviously discovered some things about
her) with an aloof stateliness. She looked like
she'd forgive, but not necessarily forget.

When Maya and Eli stepped outside, she waved
her men and her car away. "Now is Moscow's best
season. We should walk."

It must have been past 10 P.M., but the sun had

just set. As they walked over cobbled streets, Eli inhaled air thick with diesel fumes.

Maya Gorkaya still had a brisk step. After three glasses of vodka, she seemed stone cold sober. They crossed a square to an imposing old building in whose entrance Maya flashed an I.D. from her purse.

"Before Lenin," Maya said, "this was insurance company."

They passed another security checkpoint along the corridor, then reached Maya's modest office. Behind her small desk were three simply framed photos — Lenin on one end, Gorbachev on the other. In between was a pudgy angelic creature with bushy eyebrows.

"Who's that?" Eli asked.

"My patron saint. He led me to your General Powers. You know Flyorov?"

"I'm afraid I don't."

"Flyorov discovered your bomb even before you did." Perhaps Maya wasn't completely sober.

"Flyorov's superiors doubted his fission ideas because no one in the West commented. A Russian disease — we look nervously outside to confirm our own discoveries."

Maya Gorkaya seemed to be critiquing her situation as well.

"One day in the war Flyorov goes to library and sees that not only have no Americans commented on *his* ideas, but that Fermi, Teller, and other names have stopped writing—period. Flyorov knows, just as I know when General Powers disapeared from Vandenberg, that Americans are creating big. They have gone underground!"

Maya unrolled a chart on her desk. "The world of our general," she said, pointing to a Cyrillic "naypc" in the center of an inky web.

She might as well have unfurled a map of Treasure Island. Lines and arrows connected dense, meticulous script. Her plottings had a detail beyond anything Eli could imagine. Captivated, he pointed to another block of Cyrillic letters and asked, "Whose name is next to his?"

"Tanaka."

"Yuiko Tanaka?"

"Yes," Maya said, delighted. She'd found an expert sportsman obsessed with the same game. "Do you think Tanaka is a spy?"

"For a time I thought she was *you*." Eli laughed. "Is she one of yours?"

"I wish. She knows everything, but talks to no one. Personally I believe she is a Japanese sleeper."

"Sleeper?"

"Yes, quietly sleeping in a cozy place, waiting for the right moment to wake up. Within a decade, the Japanese will again be our common enemy."

As she hearkened back to the time of the Allies, Eli pointed excitedly to the name above Powers: "And this one?"

"Frank Marbles. You know him?"

"His name came up on a computer access list. And once on a message to Powers. He's Powers' boss."

"Temporarily."

"Temporarily?"

"General Powers has replaced each of his superiors. I suspect if this project succeeds, Powers will get credit. He's the man of the future. The message you glimpsed—what was it?"

"Something about a White Train leaving Pantex."

"When?"

"I don't recall." Eli's adrenaline curdled into dread. For the first moment in his career, he feared that his snooping might prove treasonous. "Where is Pantex?"

"You don't know?" Maya Gorkaya asked, astonished. "Your country lies beyond my understanding. All citizens have all information free at their fingertips and even professionals are ignorant. Pantex—all your nuclear weapons are assembled deep in the heart of Pantex, Texas. And the White Train—that is only one authorized to ship nuclear weapons. Were they shipping Raindrop to Vandenberg?"

Eli shrugged.

"If they were using that train, then they are going to test with real fire. Criminal! When do you suspect?"

"In a couple of weeks—the end of August, the very beginning of September."

"Da! Of course if we tested ours on Mayday, everyone would call us bullies. But if we claim you exploded a nuclear bomb from space on your day of labor rest, all world will call us paranoid! Where in the South Pacific will Powers do his dirty work?"

"You know as much as I do."

"In the Kwajalein atoll?"

"I have absolutely no idea. I've told you everything I know. Now I have few questions for you."

"Good, go . . ."

The door burst open: Maya's two bodyguards. They started shouting at her in Russian.

"What's happening?" Eli asked.

Maya paled. "They say you are carrying music box."

"What the hell?"

The guards seized Eli by his arms.

"Music box—radio transmitter!" Maya screamed. "Our offices pick up transmissions. Signals are beaming from your body."

The sunglasses in his vest pocket. Had they been transmitting the whole time?

22

Betrayed

"Surrender what you have!" Maya Gorkaya insisted, a metallic color returning to her face.

"What are you talking about?"

The guards started to drag Eli out of her office.

"Tell them to take their hands . . ."

Maya lunged across her desk and grabbed Eli by his collar. She yanked him back, but the guards wouldn't relax their grip. "Give it up now before I lose control of your case."

She was strangling him, yet pleading. She was pleading to be his strangler.

"Okay, okay."

Maya said something in Russian and they released their hold.

Eli reached into the vest pocket of his sports jacket and pulled out Marbles' sunglasses. "This is probably what you're looking for."

Maya grabbed the glasses and started cursing. The guards joined her. Eli thought he heard the word "Baghdad."

"You betrayed me," Maya finally said.

One guard raised his finger to his mouth and shushed her.

"Let General Powers hear!" Maya said. She held the empty glasses up to her face as if they were inhabited by an invisible head staring at her. Then she stuck out an index finger and plunged it into a lens, which popped out onto her desk.

One guard grabbed the lens and snatched the sunglasses from her.

"See what you've done to me," Maya Gorkaya shouted, then smacked Eli across the face. "I've injured State property!"

Eli sat stunned. A high-pitched ring resounded in his ears. She'd really smacked him. He said, "I demand you release me immediately."

"And next I should be reading you American rights?"

"Our conversation has ended. Take me to the American Embassy immediately."

"When did you first start working for General Powers?" Maya demanded.

"I'm not working for him now and I never have."

"Stop lying to me!" Maya shouted and started to slap him again.

Eli grabbed her arm and pinned it to the desk. "Don't touch me and don't lecture me about lying, Colonel Vera Ulyanova."

The two guards seized him again and twisted his

arms above his head until his eyes teared with pain.

"Enough already," Vera Ulyanova said. "Let him go with the innocents."

They led him down stairs that cut through the building's concrete foundation. If they were setting him free, this wasn't the likeliest route.

They opened an old iron door: an on-site prison! He bolted back toward the door. Another guard seized him. He kicked one in the legs and elbowed another in the throat. Six hands immobilized him and shoved him along the narrow passageway.

"I'm a journalist!" he shouted.

They didn't respond.

His own bastard had tricked him! Had Marbles sent him into Russia just to tape Colonel Ulyanova? Or to suffer imprisonment?

A few other prisoners edged open their cell doors and peered out. Why weren't their doors locked? They watched Eli's rite of passage with embarrassed indifference.

The guards heaved Eli into a dank cell, perhaps 6 feet by 12, with one cot, a sink and a wash basin. Or was it a urination and defecation basin?

In the corner were piles of newspapers and a stack of hard-bound books. Having just been burned, Eli immediately leafed through the books for listening devices. He found just dense pages in Russian worn by repeated reading.

Then he checked his door—locked.

A coldness descended upon him as he contemplated his situation. He sat on the cot for hours. The night passed. Perhaps the next day as well.

He thought: Suppose they let me languish? Those who know where I am don't care. And those who care don't know where I am. Marbles has seduced me into screwing myself!

He examined himself. His arms no longer hurt from either the twisting or the fire. He felt a strange, perhaps self-deceptive, calm about his ability to withstand any pain Colonel Ulyanova and her sidekicks might inflict. Oddly, he remembered glimpsing Patsy's ten-grand contribution to Amnesty International.

Hours later a succession of metal doors creaked open. He pressed his face flush against the bars of his tiny cell window and glimpsed the guards successively handing each prisoner a bowl. Soup? Stew? They also seemed to be handing out fresh newspapers. This feeding brigade approached. Then he heard the door open on the far side of his cell. They'd skipped over him.

Should he call out? Did they know he was there?

Screw them! He wasn't going to offer his captors the pleasure of a protest.

He lay down on the cot in the dank dark. He hugged himself and pretended that he wasn't there, wasn't anywhere.

Later Eli's door was opened and another prisoner shoved in. The man cursed at the guards, then rubbed his neck. A little blood rubbed off on his hand. Apparently he'd just been beaten in a crease not readily visible.

The man noticed with surprise that Eli was also in this cell. He started talking in Russian.

"I don't understand," Eli said.

"Anglish?" the beaten prisoner asked.

"American. Where are we?"

The prisoner rubbed his neck again. His wound had dried. "Hole . . . for holding *nomen* . . . for reeducating privileged."

"Great. It's an honor to be caged with the elite."

The prisoner pointed to the cot, wondering if he could sit down.

"Sure," Eli said, beckoning his cell-mate forward. "It's a free prison."

Cell doors opened down the block. Feeding time again. On this round, they opened his cell and handed in one bowl and a newspaper. Just to the other prisoner.

As soon as the door was slammed shut, Eli understood the nature of this game. Sure enough, his cell-mate offered to share the soup. Eli knocked the bowl so that its contents slopped onto the floor. "Tell Colonel Ulyanova that I'm not begging for favors."

The prisoner looked puzzled.

"Tell her!" Eli curled up on his half of the cot.

186

He didn't want to fall asleep, he couldn't afford to. He held his hands over his crotch to protect himself in case the prisoner assaulted him. He saw himself curled up in a wheelbarrow. Andy Lamkin was pushing the barrow. They were in a procession crossing a black lava moonscape. Other ghostly figures carted off other fetal bodies.

When Eli awoke, his cell-mate was gone.

23

Breaking Point

Perhaps three days passed before Colonel Ulyanova entered his cell. He was lying down on his cot. He didn't get up to greet her.

"Good morning," she said.

"I demand to see the United States Ambassador. Have you informed him or *Newsweek* that you're holding me captive?"

"You're not captive. You're just being held for questioning. But let us not get off on bad footing. I apologize for my temper. You—or should I say General Powers—caught me by surprise. And then I had to show my boys that I am business."

He stared at her as coldly as he could. Her light hair gleamed in the grayness of his cell.

"I propose a peace treaty," she said. "If we analyze our situations objectively, I believe we have much in common. Can we conduct negotiation?"

Eli sat up on the cot and placed his feet on her hard turf. "Just say what you want."

"What did Powers hope to accomplish by sending you here? Are you decoy? What kind of message are you?"

Good question, Eli thought. Pathetic that neither of them quite knew. "I already told you: Powers didn't send me. *You* sent for me. But I came with Frank Marbles' blessing."

"Marbles? Why do you think *he* blessed you?"

"So I could see who you are. He called you my dark muse. He wanted to undermine my faith in you."

"I regret his success." Vera sighed. "But that transmitter he had you bring—we have picked it apart and compared it to another confiscated from a Baathist officer who was a triple . . . such details are not important. This man's device was much older, but it transmitted a quieter signal. Speaking technologically, you were like a Sputnik. Any major nation could have picked up your signal—even the Iraqis, by example. Whoever sent you must have known you would be caught."

Alone in prison, Eli had reached this same dismal conclusion.

"And what might your capture achieve?" Colonel Ulyanova asked.

"Well, it's hard to file stories from a Moscow prison."

She chuckled. "Not to dismiss your abilities because you seem extraordinarily capable, if undisciplined. You have aggression, suspicion, intuition, perhaps principles for which you might kill. But there are easier ways to silence you. And what you know is perhaps not so extraordinary."

189

She must be trying to trick out more details. "For example?" he asked.

"You told me that soon they will test Raindrop in the South Pacific. Is this surprise? All our eyes and ears have been focused there for years. Marbles may be more afraid we are focused on our own troubles and no longer are watching. After all, what good is a weapon if the other side has no fear of it?"

"If you're so fearless now," Eli asked, "why were you so eager a week ago to learn what I knew?"

"I was tricked. As you know, the Strategic Arms Reduction Talks now proceed on many levels. Signals came that Raindrop might be quietly canceled if we offered enough. We don't have much left to give. I was convinced — by myself and others — that you could help us calculate the best offer."

"So you regarded me as a tipsheet in a secret disarmament swap?"

"I was tricked by naïveté, I confess. But at first I regarded you only as a breaking point."

"A breaking point?"

"You know: When a story breaks in *Newsweek,* maybe it is not so good as *New York Times* or your *Washington Post*. But it is certainly more convincing than *Pravda*. For the payoff you might become, I took a reasonable risk. Anyone from First Chief Directorate would appreciate that."

Colonal Ulyanova appeared to be talking to more than Eli. The prison cell must be wired. Was she building a case for herself?

"What's your point?" Eli asked abruptly.

"No more point. We can twist you for more information, but I doubt the value of what drips out."

"I'm not going to plead that I'm worth torturing."

"You see," Colonel Ulyanova leaned forward and whispered, "you and I have such concern for the future, we have stepped in old snare. Any moment now Frank Marbles may label you spy. Can you imagine how conservative American reporters will become if a prize-winner from *Newsweek* can be painted red?"

Eli *could* see the articles: "Troubled Journalist Released from Moscow Under a Cloud." Mark Lane would probably volunteer to represent him.

Colonel Ulyanova opened the cell door and gestured for Eli to follow her along the corridor. Once outside the prison's iron portal, she headed down an ancient flight of stairs.

"Where are we going?" he asked.

"If I let you out the front, anyone from either side might shoot you. I have rivals as well."

"What do they want?"

"My death. Death of disarmament. Discipline of remaining comrades. The return of old men's ways."

The stairs led to a series of vaultlike, steel doors that must have been three feet thick. After she

191

punched in the right entry codes, they entered a dark tunnel illuminated only by red lights. "This way," Vera said, hiking along a cold, concrete tunnel weeping underground dew. Where other dark tunnels intersected, elaborate steel reinforcements were visible.

"These passages—what are they for?"

"If Moscow suffers a nuclear attack, Russian leaders will find ways to survival. Do you know how old these tunnels are?"

Eli subtracted WW II from the present. "Fifty years?"

"Six hundred and fifty! Prince Donskoi dug them as soon as he defeated Tatars. The moment Russia began, we prepared for the worst. Tell Marbles and Powers we've dug deeper than they can imagine. And that to kick through clouds, we can make new galoshes."

"Galoshes?"

"They'll know what I mean."

Colonel Ulyanova and Eli came to an unmanned construction site blocking their tunnel. "We have to go aboveground because Gorbachev is reconstructing under the Kremlin wall where we bury our heroes. His work has been interrupted."

They exited up through another series of extremely thick doors to a storage vault, which led to a wing of a museum detailing the Russians' history with the Nazis. It must have been quite late because no guards or janitors were around. As they walked through the empty museum, Vera couldn't stop herself from lecturing: "The fifty years ago you mentioned, the Nazis pounded at our door. We are not an aggressive people. Can't you see that we are trying desperately to change? But if aggression is called for, we rise to occasion."

Eli couldn't figure her out. She kept threatening him with carrots, then luring him with sticks. No images fit. Vera's conspiratorial openness defied Eli's imagination. He couldn't even decide whether she was a progressive or a conservative.

As they were about to exit the museum, she warned, "My car is parked across Red Square. It's suspicious hour, but no one will bother us if we act sober."

They emerged into the vastness of Red Square. No souls were evident except the soldiers posted in front of Lenin's tomb. Yellow lights bathed the buildings inside the Kremlin. When they reached Vera's empty car, she got into the driver's seat and motioned Eli to sit alone in back.

"Help yourself to drink," Vera said, as they pulled out of Moscow

He didn't acknowledge her.

"Judge me as you wish. But if my country did not exist, your General Powers would have to invent us. He won't be satisfied until he restructures us as the enemy."

When they pulled onto the highway leading to

Sheremetyevo airport, all traffic stopped. A blockade?

Stalled in traffic, Colonel Ulyanova added, "You were a clever dangle in front of me, I confess. But what has Frank Marbles gained by exposing my weakness? I conclude that he must be desperate to show he is still top man. Russia is the medal all your Cold Warriors want to pin on their chests. Marbles must sense Powers about to seize command."

Eli stared at the motionless cars.

"Marbles is playing with you as well," Colonel Ulyanova added. "If you won't work any longer as live bait, he may try to convert you into a professional sportsman. He'll play to your reason. That's his genius."

Eli didn't respond.

The blockade turned out just to be the day's first truck breaking down. Eli stayed silent as they made their way to the airport. Again she walked him through the security checkpoints. At the departure gate she handed him a ticket to Japan.

The plane was boarding.

Eli looked directly into her translucent blue eyes as she gave a parting message: "For your record, you were never in prison, just detained for questioning. Of course we can deny or discredit whatever you print about us. But I prefer we part as respected co-investigators. The weapon system I have told you about is all too monstrous. Disclose this objective truth and you can make a difference in history. This moment for lasting peace won't come again."

Then she embraced him even more warmly than she had when he'd arrived. He couldn't believe her shamelessness. She was suggesting that they still might do business.

A primitive revulsion welled up in Eli. Had killing him seemed even slightly to Colonel Ulyanova's benefit, she wouldn't have hesitated. He shoved off her embrace.

He boarded the plane without saying a word. As it lifted toward Tokyo, Eli's thoughts flew: if neither the Americans nor the Russians can be trusted, if both are up to no good, why risk one's life to penetrate their schemes?

And yet he wondered furiously: Is Raindrop imminent? Does Bush know about it? Is disarmament really just a sideshow? Will the planet soon be bombarded by new nuclear threats?

Then he wondered about his wonderings: Did he really believe he could save the planet? No. But he wanted to be the first to sound an alarm. He was an ambulance anticipator, impelled to be at the scene of a cataclysm before it happened.

24

Called to Witness

At Tokyo passport control, a uniformed Japanese officer sat inside a thick Plexiglass booth. He held Eli's passport in his white gloves. He kept looking down at the photo and up at Eli. Surely the meticulous Japanese would discover that Eli was traveling under his brother's name. Finally the officer asked, "You have lost weight?"

"Yes."

The officer scribbled some notes on a piece of paper, then communed with his computer. The line of foreigners behind Eli kept growing. When the officer looked up again, he asked, "You have sex virus?"

AIDS! They were worried Eli had AIDS. "No — I'm a healthy, red-blooded American."

Reluctantly the Japanese officer stamped Eli's passport with a 72-hour transit visa, then crossed out the "72" and etched in a "12."

In the airport, Eli found a stopover hotel that charged by the hour. The exchange rate was terrible — sixty minutes went for twenty American dollars. And the room was a walk-in closet packed

196

with the usual amenities plus a vending machine dispensing expensive whiskey and a tiny TV monitor updating arrival and departure times.

Was Marbles really afraid of being squeezed out of the picture by Powers?

Marbles had tricked him. But if Marbles was ousted, Eli knew that he'd have to contend with a blunter instrument.

Easy instructions for international dialing were printed in six languages on a blotter next to a plastic bonsai tree. Eli dialed the McLean, Virginia, number from memory.

"CIA."

The simplicity of the greeting again stunned him.

"A message for Mr. Frank Marbles."

"In what office does he work?"

"Tell him that Eli Franklin has seen the Soviet light — or rather, its absence."

"Sir, I can't take messages. Can I . . ."

"I'm waiting at the hotel inside the Tokyo JAL terminal. Tell him that I want to be his Bill Laurence."

"Sir . . ."

"Funnel the message through PR or try Space Command," Eli said before hanging up. Then he stepped into the bathroom cubette and gazed at the mirror. He'd grown so lean that beneath a few days' stubble, he could see his cheekbones. His skin had a pallor indicative of a year, not days, in

197

a Soviet jail. No wonder the Japanese worried that his immune system was deficient.

After washing, he emerged to dial another string of numbers.

"Newsweek."

"Can I have Nina Perkin?"

"I'll put you through to her secretary."

Her secretary! When Eli first met Nina, she was a junior editorial assistant.

"Ms. Perkin's office."

"This is Eli Franklin. I'd like to speak with Nina."

"What is this in reference to?"

"I report to her. I'm a senior writer."

"Sorry, I don't know everyone's name yet. Can I take a message?"

"She's expecting my call."

"She's in a budget meeting right now and left word that she couldn't take any calls from editorial."

Editorial! The phrase inflamed Eli. "I'm not calling from editorial, I'm calling from Tokyo. I need to speak with her now."

"I'll see how much she minds being interrupted."

What seemed like fifteen minutes later Nina came to the phone. "Mr. Franklin, how nice of you to get in touch."

"I'm sorry if my timing . . ."

"Your timing's perfect. Fall off the face of the earth, then land smack in the meeting where they're testing my toughness as a budget cutter. Where the hell are you? Why Tokyo?"

"It's a long story that's going to test your credulity."

"You've already failed that test."

"Not my credibility—your credulity." Then he added, "Nina, I can't afford to fight with you. I'm near the end of a frightening story. I know the note I sent you was cryptic."

"What note?"

Christ!

"What the hell have you been doing?" she asked.

"I've discovered an American plot to station nuclear missiles in space."

"An offshoot of Star Wars?" Nina inquired, a bit curious.

"It *is* Star Wars. My source in the Soviet Union—Colonel Vera Ulyanova—claims Star Wars has been a secret offensive system from birth. The U.S. is on the verge of firing down its first test bomb."

"Eli," Nina said, her voice sobering by the second, *"Newsweek* is a mature company, do you know what that means?"

That we need a wider cut of jeans? He said, "Not exactly."

"It means we're obligated to return a steady profit to our parent corporation each year. We're not a go-go anymore. We can't afford for our reporters to take reckless fliers."

"Nina, I can't afford to stop. I'm trying to stand face to face with evil."

"Eli, we were lovers. We're still friends. Are you in some kind of drug trouble?"

"Goddammit NO!!"

"The company has good rehabilitation programs, even for employees on involuntary leave."

"Involuntary leave?"

"That's the best I could do. Wellington Steno made your case a public test. Come back into the office and we'll work everything out."

"Nina, I need money to come back. I was hoping *Newsweek* would wire me a ticket."

"I can't spend the company's money, but I'll wire some myself."

Eli needed more than money. "Nina . . ."

"You're at the Tokyo airport now, right?"

"Nina, do you believe me?"

"Of course. That's why I'm going to wire a return ticket to the United Will-Call counter. As soon as you arrive, come to my office. Do you promise?" She said this as if she were reeling in a suicidal drunk.

"I promise," he finally said. Then they both hung up.

Eli tried to muster his old rage toward *Newsweek,* toward the parent Post corporation, toward all corporations, but no anger was forthcoming. He'd gotten more leave than he deserved.

Eli punched in 15 more numbers and got a recording: "This is Patricia Geist Powers. I'm not home right now, but if you leave a message, I'll be in touch. To reach Wilson Powers, call 808-637-5011."

After the beep, Eli said: "Patsy, this is . . ."

"Eli! Hold on, I'm here!" With the tape still running, she said, "Are you all ready? I mean all right?"

"All ready for what?"

"Well . . . fabulous news: I'm pregnant!"

"Pregnant! I thought you were infertile."

"After a hundred medical tests dissecting my every part, it turns out to be Will's sperm. I was *allergic* to his sperm."

"So this is . . . do you mean *we're* pregnant?"

"I haven't slept with anyone except you and Will," Patsy said, tentatively.

Did Patsy mean that she'd only had two lovers in her entire life? Impossible. She was so experienced, so sexually mature, almost devouring.

Are you sure? he wanted to ask.

He pictured Patsy naked and was struck by her bruised beauty. She'd been subjected to tortures and trials he didn't understand. Did she want redemption with *his* baby? Or anyone's?

Eli pictured the two of them in bed together, cradling each other. "Are we ready for this?" he finally asked.

"I am." Her voice was equal parts resolve and anxiety. "But you can be as uninvolved as you want."

"I want to be involved!" The passion in his own voice unnerved him. "When did all this happen?"

"The results came last week. It must have happened in your cabin, right after our date in Santa Cruz."

Eli remembered how irresistible she'd seemed. He'd given in to his giddy feelings and then all hell broke loose. "How are you feeling?" he asked.

"Wonderful! Except I'm sleeping all the time. I'm blissfully oblivious to practically everyone and everything except smell. Then it's as if I'm an animal sniffing out danger."

"My God, what does Will think?"

"He doesn't think anything. He doesn't need to know. He's still fighting the divorce and there's no sense complicating matters. Surely this information, as he'd say, is on a need-to-know basis."

Eli envisioned a tape machine recording their every word. Would Marbles or Powers be in charge of the tap? Bank on Marbles—and undermine this bank at the same time. "Patsy, have you ever heard of Frank Marbles?"

"Of course. He came over for dinner when we lived down at Vandenberg. Quite a brilliant man."

"Did Will tell you Marbles was his boss?"

"He just said they worked together."

"Did Will look up to him?"

202

"Does Will look up to anyone?"

"What did Will say after Marbles left?" Eli asked, like an attorney leading a key witness.

Patsy paused. "He chastised me for flirting. I wasn't flirting, I was just trying to feel alive. But Will was jealous beyond reason. He feeds on rivals."

The beep whined, indicating that at least Patricia's tape had run its course. Eli said that he wouldn't entangle her in any more details, but that he'd be back for good as soon as he finished his infernal story.

"Whatever troubles you may be in," Patsy said before hanging up, "don't think I'm oblivious to them. And remember you have more courage than you know. I trust your instincts. I'm joining forces with them."

Eli unfurled the futon. When he lay down for a rest, he fell into a courtroom where there were two General Powerses — Powers as the D.A. and Powers as the judge. His own attorney was in the dark. Could anyone beat this system?

Someone was rapping a gavel on his head. He opened his eyes — the digital clock in his room indicated that he'd slept 15 hours. Someone was still rapping. Must be the Japanese hotelier telling him he'd overstayed his welcome.

"I'm coming," he said, walking naked to the door.

He opened the door slightly.

The husky Melanesian. The one who'd tailed him in San Jose. The messenger.

"Mr. Marbles was taken by your message," Ratu said. "You're invited to witness his fireworks."

25

Stranger in Paradise

Ratu escorted Eli through the Tokyo airport with a disturbing jauntiness.

"Where are we going?" Eli asked.

Ratu pointed to the "Nadi, Fiji" boarding gate sign. "Do I look like a hijacker?"

Perhaps. In Ratu's presence, Eli felt as if he were under heavily armed guard. After the plane took off, Eli asked, "Is Ratu your first or last name?"

"Ratu is Fijian for 'Lord.' Mr. Marbles pays me honor with this joke."

"Americans! What a friendly way to take someone down a notch."

"Don't provoke me."

"I'm serious," Eli said, trying to determine his own status. Infiltrator or captive? "I'm considering working for Marbles myself. Does he ask you to do his dirty work?"

"He's become a soft boss. He doesn't ask me to do enough." Ratu buried his attention in a *Sports Illustrated*.

As they were landing, Eli made one final stab. "So how did they recruit you?"

"I did the recruiting. Mr. Marbles helped rid our land of Indians."

Eli had visions of the CIA cavalry driving out Apaches, but when they disembarked on Fiji, he saw throngs of Asian Indian women sobbing goodbye to their men. A coup—Eli vaguely remembered. Indigenous Fijians had ousted an Indian, anti-nuclear party elected to power. What price were the natives now paying for the CIA's aid?

A vendor passed by, peddling oranges larger than grapefruits. Eli handed over an American dollar. No question was asked, no change given. As he was eating the orange, a familiar voice said, "Has Ratu been sharing the fruits of his country?"

A glistening bald dome accented by a meticulously trimmed mustache and goatee. Perhaps 70, but seemingly toughened by age. The only anticipated resemblance to Eli's old Professor Trilling were Marbles' world-weary eyes.

Frank Marbles extended his hand. Eli's were clearly full of orange sections and peels. Even Marbles' initial gesture contained a put-down.

Eli put down the peels and shook hands.

"Shall we get going?" Marbles said immediately. "We're in quite a rush."

The three of them marched along the tarmac. Eli realized he had to take the offensive. His credibility and probably his life were at stake. If he hid his rage, Marbles would be doubly suspicious. Some sort of ride seemed certain, but doubtless Marbles was still deciding at what level he should risk taking Eli on board.

Above the din of jumbo jets Eli said, "Don't think I've forgotten that you deceived me. You sent me into Russia bleating electronically."

"If I'd been leading you to slaughter, you'd be dead now. Believe me."

They reached a black plane that looked like a cross between a corporate sportster and a stealth fighter jet. When Marbles turned, his eyes were in the shadow of his own face. He looked like a blind priest. He said to Eli, "Sit up front with me."

"You're a pilot?"

"Since the Second War. And no one has ever accused me of bailing out too soon."

Ratu climbed without comment into the pressurized cargo bay. Eli followed Marbles up a metal ladder into the small cockpit and sat in the copilot's seat.

Marbles flipped a few switches: The ladder retracted, the cockpit sealed and all the electronic displays came alive in digital readouts. Marbles taxied onto the runway, told the control tower he was ready, then made a steeply inclined takeoff.

Two high resolution video screens were embedded into the instrument panel. Each had rounded edges like an old-fashioned television set, but their pictures conveyed 3-D depth. The screen in front of Marbles displayed an evolving navigation map. On the monitor in front of Eli, a topographic likeness of Fiji labeled "Main Island" dwindled away.

"Under your seat is a souvenir," Marbles said.

Eli fished out a manila envelope. Inside was a 8 x 10 glossy photo of Eli shoving off Vera Ulyanova's embrace!

"How did you get this?"

"*Glasnost* presents its photo opportunities."

When Eli started to put the glossy back under his seat, Marbles said, "Keep it. I already sent copies to all the boys betting she'd get *my* hide!"

"Has she targeted you as well as Powers?"

"I'm her *main* target. She knows I'm the mastermind, doesn't she?"

Marbles' nervous bragging braced Eli. "Colonel Ulyanova doesn't know what to think. She's not sure whether you're trying to conceal the Black Hole or rub her nose in it."

"Shrewd. Lucky her scientists aren't as clever."

"But she hinted that the Soviets are also developing space-based missiles."

"If they were as close as we are, they wouldn't have grasped so desperately for you," Marbles said with a condescension intended to make Eli feel insignificant.

They climbed high above the clouds. The transparent bubble surrounding the cockpit afforded them command of the skies. Marbles punched a plan into what looked like a computerized automatic pilot and turned on a device labeled "The Shadow Box." Then he asked, "What do you know about Bill Laurence?"

"He was the first journalist to describe the atom bomb."

"More than describe it! By comparing atomic power to the Second Coming of Christ, he made Americans understand that we'd bombed for peace. We brought Laurence onto the Manhattan Project's ground floor. Months before Truman understood what was going on, Bill Laurence conceived the words that would come out of the President's mouth."

Marbles was making Eli an offer.

Eli asked, "Would you say that, technologically speaking, you're working on the Third Coming?"

"*You* could say that more convincingly than I ever could. And you'd be right. And remembered. Someone is going to tell the story of the tiny weapon that won the arms race."

The screen in front of Marbles said, "Designated Landing Site — 100 miles."

"So you don't believe in disarmament?" Eli asked.

"Mutual public relations. Both sides get rid of obsolete weapons and the world applauds. I'm not saying this isn't a time of great opportunity."

They descended upon a black and green speck. Marbles landed the jet along a strip that paralleled the island's lone mountain. Two Fijians as husky as Ratu drove a flatbed truck out to greet them. After unloading Ratu and several crates from the plane's belly, the five of them rumbled over a cinder road to an abandoned construction site. "ParadiseWorld" signs were posted everywhere.

When they parked in a dried lagoon basin encrusted with lava-mache rocks, Marbles explained: "Americans were developing this property. Then they got caught up in a leveraged buyout and nearly sold it to the Japanese." His tone had stiffened, as if to warn Eli to hold questions until no other nationalities were present.

One of the Fijians unpacked a box containing sandwiches. The other neatly sealed crates had Cupertino, CA., Austin, TX. and Framingham, MA. return addresses. Ratu drove off with these. A sophisticated control or monitoring station must be hidden in the half-finished resort.

As they ate roast beef on sourdough and sipped beer, Marbles chatted about recent rugby results with the Fijians, who were named Cako and Mike. When Ratu returned, Marbles pulled out a packet from his flight suit. "Green kava, my friends."

He neatly tore off the top of the packet, poured the powder into a USAF canteen and shook it up.

Ratu watched Marbles intently. "*You* drink first," he said.

Marbles took a deep swig. Then he poured a little brown puddle into his palm and drank this as well. "Our factory's best pickle juice, I can assure you."

Why was Marbles reassuring Ratu? Something was nagging Eli—a misplaced phone number from another life. Meanwhile the Fijians built a small fire and peacefully watched its flames.

"Let's go for a walk," Marbles suggested to Eli as the sun set. "A leadership conference."

Marbles led Eli past portable latrines and an occasional building frame. ParadiseWorld looked like an archeological site. The dug-up ground had been divided by construction forms, but not much concrete had been poured. Brackish water had seeped into the man-made cavities, rusting the reinforcing steel bars that lay in heaps like excavated javelins.

"Let's climb," Marbles said as they reached a gravel path leading upward. "You look like the kind of chap who enjoys an overview."

The path paralleled a slope that had been bulldozed smooth. "Was this going to be a golf course?" Eli asked.

"Good eye. After the Americans went belly-up, the Japanese wanted to landscape the entire course with rock gardens."

Eli ventured further: "General Powers seems to have an interest in things Japanese."

"You've noticed that?"

"I'm not the only one. As you *overheard,* Colonel Ulyanova thinks his Ms. Tanaka is a Japanese sleeper."

"Ulyanova feeds on her paranoia. That's practically the only food the Russians have left. But just to be on the safe side, when we return I'm going to analyze Ms. Tanaka's comings and goings on my TRIPSEARCH."

Marbles ignored Eli's contemptuous emphasis of "overheard." Suggesting that bygones be bygones, he was inviting Eli into his world.

211

26

The High Road

"TRIPSEARCH?" Eli asked as he hurried to catch up with Marbles on the hard gravel path.

"A little program I have that tracks the trips my employees take, sorting out suspicious patterns to Mexico City, Vienna, that sort of thing."

A modern tool for an old mind-set, Eli thought. Then asked, "How many employees do you have?"

Marbles kept climbing. "Are subcontractors employees? Is the mechanic who maintains my plane an employee? Anyway, I'm just overseeing certain aspects of this research."

Marbles said this with total insincerity and poorly concealed pride.

"How many would you guess?"

"I enjoy guessing games. But you go first. How many people were employed by the Manhattan Project? Come close and I'll answer your question."

"Five thousand?"

"A little off. Want to guess again?" Marbles' patronizing tone suggested to Eli that he was far from the mark. Marbles wanted to show that historic projects devoured manpower.

"Fifty thousand," Eli shot back.

"One hundred fifty thousand. Of course only a dozen people oversaw the whole shebang. I know because I wasn't one of them. When I reached a position to know, I retrospectively examined the bigot list."

A gourmet tidbit. Marbles was teasing Eli's appetite. "What's a bigot list?" Eli asked.

" 'Bigot' meaning narrow — only those privileged to know."

A half moon had risen in the sky. Its top half seemed so luminous and its bottom so utterly invisible that it was hard to credit it as a sphere. The moon looked as if it had lost its ballast and naturally levitated.

"By 1940," Marbles continued, "even the French, the Italians and the Danes had insights about atomic fission. But only the U.S. threw its entire industrial might behind the project."

"Nice to have resources at your command."

"The Germans, the Japanese and the Soviets had sufficient resources. All they lacked was courage to seize the future."

Marbles stopped, zipped open his jumpsuit and peed off the side of the path. As Eli joined him, he remembered Colonel Ulyanova's whisper about old snares.

"When Colonel Ulyanova was defending herself," Eli said. "She claimed, 'Anyone from the First Chief Directorate would appreciate risks I've taken.' I had the feeling she was talking to more than just me."

"Shrewd." Marbles continued striding uphill. The half-moon cast elongated shadows behind them. "She was reminding anyone listening of her ties to Vladimir Alexandrovich Kryuchov. Before he became chairman of the KGB, Kryuchov headed this Directorate."

"Which is?"

"Responsible for all foreign spying. It's an elite unit, which is why other Directorates are collecting its mistakes for the day of deadly reckoning, a day coming sooner than anyone dared imagine."

Marbles climbed at an amazing pace for a 70-year-old. He asked, "How many employees do you imagine work for the KGB chairman?"

"Give me a clue. How many currently work for the CIA?"

"Left wing estimates would put the number at twenty thousand."

"Twenty thousand employees times ten. Two hundred thousand."

"Closer than last time. A third of the way there."

"Six hundred thousand KGB agents! You expect me to swallow that?"

"Admittedly one hundred and fifty thousand of these are just technical support staff, and three hundred and fifty thousand troops and border guards. But you get my point."

"That they're a bloated enemy."

Marbles laughed. "I'm enjoying our conversation. This bloat is precisely the reason Gorbachev ordered Kryuchov to shift resources in Colonel Ulyanova's direction. The Communists can no longer afford internal repression and they can't survive without it. So they've been forced to become more efficient."

"How deep is her support?"

"From an external security standpoint, one spymaster focusing on technology is worth ten thousand clerks or border guards. Or border countries, for that matter. That's why Ulyanova may survive my little humiliation. By the way, how well did she take everything?"

Eli didn't know whether to play his Powers' card yet — Ulyanova's conviction that Marbles' chief subordinate was destined to supplant him. "She's tricky to read," Eli said, turning his gaze back down to the Fijians. Their campfire had dwindled to a small glow in the distance.

As the path changed from hard gravel to loose rock, Marbles trudged ahead.

"So what does President Bush think of your project?" Eli asked.

"He doesn't need to think anything."

"That was Reagan's style. Surely you must have ties to Bush from his days at the CIA?"

"Oh, he's supportive of our strategic goals, if that's what you're asking. Like the other nine Presidents I've served, he knows that the world is full of unpleasant realities and . . ." Marbles stopped short of breath. "Quite a good view here."

This high up the mountain, the shore seemed like a hemline at their feet. The Pacific and Southern night sky stretched out before them. Distant clouds resting on the horizon looked like far-off mountains. Eli was reminded of his winter run on the summit of the Santa Cruz mountains, when he couldn't exactly tell where the ocean ended and the atmosphere began.

Marbles smoothed out the gravel and sat down. No

plateau was evident at this point on the path. Di[d]
Marbles want to slow down the questioning? Perhap[s]
offer a sympathetic glimpse behind his contemptuou[s]
mask? From experience, Eli knew that even celebritie[s]
found their personas tiresome.

"What's the most unpleasant reality about you[r]
work?" Eli asked, sitting.

"Well, you have to assume the worst. That's you[r]
job. Or if you're good, your mission. But if you're n[o]
careful, you can become so infatuated with negativ[e]
possibilities that you help create them."

"Copulating with destruction?"

"That's the danger. You need to remember your ini[-]
tial aim."

"Which was?"

"To make the Soviets think thrice before contem[-]
plating something nasty. You may be surprised t[o]
learn that Eisenhower started this targeting strategy[.]

"Targeting?"

"Make them worried about their own skins[.]
Whether it's a tin-pot dictator or a Kremlin kingpin[,]
that's all the bad guys finally care about."

"And the good guys?"

"I admit we have our own self-serving elements[,]
whiz kids infatuated with weapons for their ow[n]
sake."

"So who does Bush listen to?"

"As far as honor is concerned, the President is fro[m]
the old school. But he's also a fan of the new competi[-]
tive strategies."

"Could you use a little publicity to secure his atten[-]
tion?"

216

"Let's cut the crap."

Eli felt suddenly exposed. He started to shiver. The tropical breeze had tuned brisk at this atmosphere. "Before we continue our discussion, perhaps you might tell me what will happen if I don't sympathize with you."

"I'm not threatening you."

"But Powers is."

"I've warned Powers that you're under my control now."

"And how controllable is *he?*"

"You and I both recognize that he enjoys overkill. In his world, one gains strength through perpetual conflict. *I* only want an arsenal to enforce peace, which I suspect you can appreciate. But if you don't, so be it. The truth is: I'm not terribly worried about any exposé you may have in mind."

"And why is that?" Eli said as confidently as he could.

"Whatever the details of your deal with *Newsweek's* assistant executive editor, any article you propose isn't likely to see print."

"Why is *that?*"

"You have no standing in this field."

Pissed, Eli rose to his feet.

"Don't be so literal." Marbles tugged him back down. "You know all military stories emanate from official sources. But *Newsweek* isn't even a major outlet, except for damage control. We used *Time's* Washington bureau recently to rectify a misleading story. It wouldn't take much to enlist your Washington bureau to provide similar support. They'd see any

217

exposé you proposed as an attack on their mandate. And it would be. Their job isn't to break news, but to summarize what's been announced and leaked the previous week. Am I saying anything you don't know?"

He wasn't. Marbles seemed at home in the cold atmosphere, as if he were a fallen archangel.

"Even if you did manage to get a little story in print, who would run with it? The networks follow the *Times,* the *Post,* occasionally the *Journal.* Do you really think that the *Post* would pick up on your piece? They regard *Newsweek* as a clipping service."

"What are you proposing?" Eli asked.

"Nothing so crude as censorship or propaganda — just that you let me help you build your standing in a professional way."

"And how would you help me do that?"

"Just like on this walk. I'll feed you tips, steer you in the right direction."

"For example?"

"The KGB's refurbished Bykovo where Colonel Ulyanova was schooled. They're scrapping their occupation forces, but modernizing their espionage training. Who do you think placed your ticket in that Coke can? They're littering America with spies now. Did you know that each agent has to develop a personal sports legend?"

"A what?"

"Say an agent's destination is the East Coast, he might develop a history as a suffering Red Sox fan. Engineers about to be placed in Silicon Valley study the rise of the 49ers. I can show you a page from their

218

curriculum: 'How to let down one's guard with colleagues.' An agent might learn to admit, after a few beers, to a period when he doubted Joe Montana."

"An amusing back of the book story. An end-of-the-era piece."

"Which would build your credibility for the next era," Marbles said, rising. The clouds from the horizon had now reached and obscured the half-moon. The backlit sky seemed ominous, as if something larger than a reflective satellite were behind it. "It's getting dark. Let's start down."

"And when would it be appropriate for the Raindrop story to appear?" Eli asked.

"When we've done more tests; decided on orbits, yields delayed, fuses. One of these days the country is going to get a military wake-up call that's going to change the public atmosphere. When we have something a lot bigger than Grenada under our belt, we can sell Congress on the need for more aggressive defense. Right now we're just R&D at the tip of the new single integrated operations plan. You'll never get any confirmation that anything exists."

The trip down was harder going than the climb up. Eli had to keep his eyes fixed on his feet so that he wouldn't twist an ankle. Watching his big feet wade down the rocky slope brought to mind another of Ulyanova's comments.

"Colonel Ulyanova also gave me a warning about making new galoshes."

"She caught the wit in 'Raindrop.' "

"What was she talking about?"

"Galosh is the name of the missile the Russians use

to protect Moscow. One ABM system is permitted under the 1972 treaty. But galoshes are useless for hitting incoming multiple warheads. That's why they're secretly modifying theirs so that they can shoot down low-orbiting satellites. And of course they're working on high-energy laser weapons. Ulyanova was threatening a preemptive strike on Raindrop."

Marbles seemed reinvigorated by this threat. "Someday she could be a formidable opponent. She's just got to learn the rules of the game. I hope she doesn't go after me personally first. I'd find out, of course."

They reached the campfire. The Fijians were staring at waning embers. Eli followed Marbles twenty yards away from the fire, where they both climbed into USAF sleeping bags. The sky above them had cleared, revealing clouds of stars. Or were they galaxies? Distant ellipses retreated from view. Eli fell asleep clinging to his small orb, twirling in space.

27

When Evil Explodes

Before sunrise the next morning Marbles roused Eli. Holding up a bony index finger so that it bisected his manicured mustache and goatee, Marbles urged Eli not to wake anyone. The two of them tiptoed in the predawn twilight to the truck.

"What about the others?" Eli asked as they headed safely to the airfield.

"Ratu will wake them shortly and have them man their station. He's been briefed on their duties. Assuming everything goes right, we'll be back on the ground in a few hours."

"Assuming what goes right?"

"We're shooting from space into the barrel this morning."

"Where's the barrel?" Eli asked as they rumbled over the cinder road.

"The crater up there." Marbles pointed to the mountaintop, which seemed almost touchable. It peaked perhaps four miles away.

"You're going to fire a missile at *this* island!"

"The Russians have nuclear devices seeded

221

throughout their earthquake regions." Marbles' face beamed. "As soon as a quake happens — Boom! Even after Armenia, they immediately tested a nuclear device. For years now, our stations in places like Alaska, Korea, China, Turkey and Norway have tricked out the differences between their natural and unnatural seismic waves."

"You're kidding?"

"Absolutely not. They've coupled their mischief with decoupling techniques — detonations in hollowed-out chambers that muffle explosions so they appear to be innocent Rayleigh or Love waves."

Although he hadn't drunk kava the previous night, Eli's brain felt groggy. "What does this island have to do with earthquakes?"

"It's a dormant volcano. We're not about to bomb this baby with nuclear fire, but we've got a new EPW with an ultrastrength metal warhead."

"EPW?"

"Earth Penetrating Weapon. It burrows deep into the underground. The Kremlin will go wild imagining what we've tested."

"Weren't you shipping a nuclear device on the White Express?"

"Just practicing for the future. I believe in playing hoaxes to the hilt."

Eli slunk into his passenger seat. "So which is it? Are you trying to threaten the Soviets into military submission? Or are you goading them to chase after you?"

"Both." Marbles picked up the speed. "And the beauty is Gorbachev can't protest publicly. Disarmament is his baby. If it dies, he's brought his people nothing but grief."

As Eli bounced, he pictured the island shaking after an explosion. He knew little about volcanoes, but he couldn't imagine that even a dormant one would appreciate a ballistic enema. "Don't you ever worry about tempting the gods?"

"You went to an Ivy," Marbles pressed on. "Didn't you dissect the classics? Man *is* Prometheus. We created the god Prometheus the day we discovered fire. Love of new sparks is what makes us human *and* god-like."

"And the fire this time is a bigger bomb?"

"That's the other beauty. To pin down the Russian elite — or any other elite — from the edge of space, you only need elite warheads. Smart, tiny ones that can penetrate into our enemies' brain cells. When the time comes, we can sell this entire program as 21st-century disarmament."

"Meanwhile the more anxious you make the Kremlin about Raindrop, the more resources they'll pour into their underground shelters and counterpart weapons?"

"Exactly."

"And the more money they waste on defense?"

"The emptier their food shelves. As poor Gorbachev understands, that's the real bomb ticking away in their midst."

They reached the airstrip. Marbles climbed out and Eli followed after him. "What if your scheme backfires?"

"Making Moscow chase our military technology is

the best way to finally bankrupt their bankrupt system. We're entering their make-or-break year."

"Which would you prefer?"

"Why settle for coexistence when you can have surrender? We can enforce a new world order when we have the high ground to ourselves."

Marbles turned toward his plane and gestured for Eli to join him. "C'mon, I'll answer all your questions once we're aloft. You'll have a front-row seat that would make Bill Laurence die of envy."

"But what if you miss the target?" Eli persisted.

"We won't miss. Even with a partial success, this program will be in the pipeline when the next funding cycle begins. That's why everyone in Defense is pulling for us."

"Everyone? You hinted last night about your rivals."

"No question that the other services resent what goes on behind the Air Forces's Blue Curtain of Secrecy."

"I meant rivals *within* your project."

"There are always rivals for credit. But even superfast burners like Powers understand the need to cooperate now."

"If your aim is guaranteed, why don't we stay on the ground to observe?"

"I don't have time for this!" Marbles shouted as he hurried toward the plane. "Remember: This is just a test. No one's committed yet to using this weapon."

Eli hesitated. He was repulsed by Marbles' logic. To join Marbles aloft was to cross over into complicity.

Besides, why was Marbles leaving the Fijians behind? Eli pictured them climbing out of their sleeping bags — and saw their faces pockmarked with purple measles. Might their presence at ground level be a medical part of the test? But if Eli stayed behind, he'd also be exposed.

When Marbles reached the plane's ladder, he turned back toward the frozen Eli. "What's the matter? Did Ulyanova chop off your pecker in her prison?"

"I'm not afraid of her," Eli said, not moving. He felt frightened of everything.

Marbles looked disappointed. Wordlessly he ascended the ladder and retracted it. Before sealing the cockpit, he yelled back, "I took a big chance with you. You're dying to see how elites really work, but you're afraid to join forces with any side. You're doomed to be a spectator!"

Eli stood forlorn on the runway as the plane took off with an almost vertical ascent. He thought, "My questions were naive, my strategy nil, my insights impotent."

Marbles' plane climbed above the volcano's peak into the pink dawn. Suddenly the plane burst at its center and flung all its flaming parts toward the sea.

Colonel Ulyanova had shot down Marbles' plane! Or Powers?

Before Eli could decide, a chalk line streaked down from the heavens into the flank of the volcano. Raindrop! At the moment of impact, a phenomenal white light obliterated all color from the sky. All everything.

Then the ground beneath Eli thundered.

28

Point Blank

Eli steadied himself against the truck. Seconds later a profounder detonation forced him to his knees as everything on the island, including the truck, started percolating.

If the volcano's old crater was the intended bull's-eye, the missile had missed by perhaps a quarter of a mile. Lava began spouting from the gash opened high on the slope. Several thin streams of molten rock rolled seaward.

The lava followed the path of least resistance: the bulldozed fairways that sloped down to Paradise-World. Whatever their complicity, Ratu and his sidekicks deserved a warning. Eli mounted the truck and drove back.

The ground rose and fell slightly before Eli's eyes. He slowed so that the truck could handle the bulges. At a crawl, he felt aftershocks — sudden kicks. The island was behaving as if it were pregnant with a disturbed child.

When he reached PardiseWorld, he yelled, "Ratu!"

No answer. Driving amid the naked excavations, he found all three men in a roofless hut facing an Olympic-size swimming pool basin. They were overseeing equipment in the shell of a refreshment stand.

Eli's appearance seemed to horrify Ratu even more than the island's convulsions.

Ratu believes I should be dead, Eli thought. *He sabotaged Marbles' plane.*

Meanwhile the steel-encased, high-tech instruments happily registered the havoc. Ratu's partners observed the electronic numbers mount, the oscilloscopes fluctuate, the titanium needles wag. This struck Eli as mere display: all these instruments clearly had internal recording devices. They were designed to function automatically near ground zero and transmit their findings elsewhere.

"We're guinea pigs!" Eli shouted. "Let's get out of here!"

Cako and Mike turned to Ratu, who still looked as if a ghost were confronting him.

Again Eli shouted, "Let's get out of here!" He hurried back toward the truck and the Fijians reluctantly followed. When he entered the cab, they climbed onto the flatbed. Eli drove toward the shore. Wispy clouds thickened into a warm fog. A roar resounded above the crash of waves. What was happening?

Eli parked the truck and climbed up to a bluff overlooking the ocean. Ratu followed him.

Atop the cliff, Eli peered through the steamy uproar. Several rivers of fire emerged at the shore only to be extinguished by waves. Then the flames reignited.

Magma must be racing underground from the bomb site to the sea. Eli had driven to the shore in an attempt to flee danger. In fact, he'd taken his party to the edge.

The perpetual marriage of fire and water was the most astounding spectacle Eli had ever seen. After the waves doused the fire, black fingers of new land arose. Then fire seeped out from these new black nails. Flaming hands were fighting to grab hold of the ocean.

Eli inhaled the white steam drifting upward: sweet with a hint of sulfur. Was this perfume radioactive? Had Marbles lied about the nature of the test? Or was he deceived?

Eli turned to Ratu, on whose face dozens of tiny sweat beads now emerged. "When Powers gave you the explosive device to plant aboard Marbles' plane, did he tell you whether Raindrop would be nuclear?"

"I don't know what you're talking about. Stop talking."

"When Powers hired you as his goon," Eli repeated sarcastically, "did he warn you that you'd be playing with poison?"

"I didn't poison anyone," Ratu insisted. "Powers just asked me to distract him."

"Distract who?"

"Nobody."

The word "nobody" ignited in Eli's head. Reignited. Who was a nobody?

"What was this nobody's name?" Eli demanded.

"I don't know any names. The general didn't tell me he'd have a baby girl with him."

A baby girl? Impossible!

Eli accused Ratu as hatefully as he could: "You

poisoned Andy Lamkin, didn't you?"

"I never said that. Never said anything." Ratu drew a handgun from his pocket. "He died in an accident."

"Sweet Jesus!" Eli said, ignoring the gun.

Ratu aimed the gun at Eli. "General Powers knew you planned to turn us in. He said Marbles had joined you on the other side—joined the fools who believe in peace through weakness."

Ratu was daring Eli to attack. Or was he justifying what was about to be a quick murder?

Eli glanced at Cako and Mike, who were waiting below. Watching the clash of forces.

Ratu extended his burly arm toward Eli's face. He was concentrating his 250 pounds to squeeze the trigger.

Eli felt a cold black rage erupting in him. He hadn't come this far to be extinguished like a nobody.

Ratu's feet were firmly planted in the ground. If Eli shoved him, Ratu was ready to shrug off the assault.

"You're right, I don't worship strength," Eli said, lunging forward. The adrenaline fueling his lunge also magnified his perceptions. Time turned cool. In what seemed like slow motion, he twisted Ratu's trigger hand toward the land.

As Eli had hoped, Ratu exerted a tremendous counterforce to jerk back his hand. Eli slipped his leg behind Ratu and aided Ratu's force. By his own exertion, Ratu fell backward over the cliff, firing helplessly into the air.

Eli pulled away until the shots ceased. Then he peeked over the edge of the cliff. He winced. Ratu's body washed back and forth at the surf's edge as if he

229

were a beached baby whale.

Cako and Mike came up to see.

Eli thought: It was self-defense. I'll make sure they confirm that immediately. Instead he said, "If either of you mess with me, you'll be just as dead. Now how the fuck can we get out of here?"

"There's a boat down in the cove," Mike replied.

"How long will it take us to get back to the main island?"

"Maybe a couple of days."

The 30-foot Boston Whaler with a ParadiseWorld insignia had apparently been intended for snorkling trips once the resort was finished. Without exchanging words, Cako and Mike launched the boat. Eli stayed in the bow seat staring out into the ocean. He didn't look back for fear he might again see Ratu's body.

As the ocean sprayed his face, Eli ruminated: Why did Powers kill Marbles? Because he thought he could get away with it. Once Raindrop was successfully tested, it would pass beyond its intelligence phase and revert to the military. Even Marbles sensed that he was being used as deep cover inside the Black Hole. He was part of the hoax being played to the hilt. But he wasn't ready to abdicate control.

Because command would now pass unequivocally to Powers, Marbles' death wouldn't be excessively investigated. Powers would blame it on shock waves from the test. Or on Colonel Ulyanova.

Ulyanova. Marbles' murder was a message to her as

well. And to her superiors. Powers was confirming their worst suspicions: he was a brute who'd strike wherever and whomever he wished. Powers thrived on this reputation. Secretly America did as well. The Pentagon was privately warning the Kremlin that Star Wars was a deadly game they had to play even as their empire unraveled. Race after us or your own existence will be at risk.

And Ratu? Powers couldn't possibly let a simple goon remain alive—he was linked to the murders. Eli turned to the other Fijians. "Did Ratu say you'd be leaving the test island on this boat?"

"He said someone else would get us in a week," Mike replied.

Powers was keeping his options alive. He'd receive electronic confirmation that Marbles' plane had exploded and would assume that Eli had been aboard. Even if Powers feared otherwise, he'd have no way of knowing.

Being reduced to an afterthought gave Eli a head start—a week to get this story into print.

Excited, Eli realized that he'd stopping thinking about Ratu's lifeless body. Powers would certainly have killed Ratu anyway.

"When we get back to the main island," Eli warned Cako and Mike, "you'd better disappear. Hide out in a village. If you tell anyone what happened to Ratu or me, you'll be murdered. Do you understand?" Eli stared at them until they saw he was deadly serious.

Then he turned his back and continued gazing out from the prow. If Cako and Mike attacked him, Eli felt he could kill them with his bare hands. For the

231

moment, Eli believed he could summon whatever force was necessary.

Their vessel took all seas with indifference — sometimes they glided over glassy waters, sometimes they crashed through whitecaps. Eli's new strength had an indifferent prow as well. If he hoped to beat General Powers, he couldn't afford to agonize about Ratu's or Marbles' or anyone else's fate.

A dark thought surfaced: he'd lost *and* discovered a part of himself in the Black Hole.

29

Publish or Perish

When they reached Fiji's main island, Eli managed to transfer electronically the ticket Nina had wired to the Tokyo airport. Under a false name, he flew to Los Angeles, then immediately took the red-eye to New York so that he could rush into print.

Where should Eli strike? Where was Powers vulnerable? If Eli managed to provoke a Congressional investigation of Raindrop, Powers had the perfect fall guy. "My superior Marbles assured me that all our actions had been approved." An Air Force Academy valedictorian and a chief of operations at Vandenberg could cite case after honorable case of previously obeying orders.

Descending into JFK, Eli wondered why Patsy had married Powers. Her initial attraction to him was forgivable. Probably when he was on sabbatical at Stanford's Business School, he'd been at his most relaxed. He was athletic, handsome, smart. And her father's endorsement counted for something. But what was *her* desire? Why did she marry someone who'd spent a lifetime achieving the conditions that would let him get away with murder?

As the plane touched down, Eli felt relieved that he didn't have to call Patsy yet. He couldn't do a single thing in the next few days that might tip off Powers.

On the cab ride in, as they passed Shea Stadium, the driver asked Eli in singsong English, "Sir, can you believe those fawking Mets?"

"Easily," Eli said.

The driver appeared Indonesian. Eli had circled the world only to be ferried the last miles home by an immigrant who'd journeyed the opposite way.

They hit some familiar road construction. A few workers were drinking their coffee beside a sealed hole. Today looked like their last day on the project. Or perhaps their first. It hardly mattered. Con Ed, the telephone company, assorted pavers and pipefitters and middlemen had conspired for years to dig for public dollars at the same old holes. In such a mood Eli returned to the Upper West Side.

His sublessees were long gone. They'd left his co-op so clean it looked as if it were up for sale. Eli wondered how much a top floor, spacious 1 BR pre-war w. parquet floors and molding and a working WBF would go for in today's market. Assessing their property's value helped New Yorkers feel better about all the living compromises they'd been forced to make.

Eli disrobed quickly and stepped into the shower. He wanted to get into work immediately. For a minute, the water was invigorating, then the temperature and pressure dropped. As his neighbors began

234

their morning ablutions, the plumbing arteries of his prewar building showed their age.

Opening his closet, Eli reached for his gray pin-striped suit. No, on an Indian summer day, it would seem uptight. He grabbed a silk tan. No, he didn't want to look as if he'd been on an extended vacation. He settled on a dark weave from Italy. Turning, he knocked over his bedroom floor lamp. Christ, he didn't even know where things stood in his own apartment. He picked up the lamp and smacked it down on the floor, denting the parquet.

He disembarked from his second cab of the day at Fifth and 50th. He always walked the final block to work down the aisle between St. Patrick's and Saks. In front of 444 Madison, as he glanced up from the sidewalk, the *Newsweek* building looked like an old castle. Entering the lobby, he was relieved when the building guard didn't acknowledge or detain him. And that he knew no one on his ride up to the tenth floor.

He turned briskly toward the southwest flank to avoid encountering colleagues. His key still worked! His office was like his co-op: someone had worked here in his absence, but they'd left the place clean. Cautiously he checked each of his desk and file drawers to make sure Powers hadn't planted a welcoming present.

He felt more panicked now than his first day on the job. Coming over from the *Voice,* Eli had acted as if he already knew all their trade's tricks. With this cosmopolitan bravado, he'd pleased everyone except the angry prophet inside himself.

He dialed Nina's extension.

"Eli! Where are you?"

"Back in my office."

"Terrific! I'm free. You can come up right now."

Eli took the back stairs, which allowed passage up to the twelfth, *Newsweek*'s other editorial floor. These were perhaps the last set of stairs in the security-conscious building that allowed anything beyond an emergency exit.

Nina hadn't said exactly where her new office was located, but the "You can come up" was more than enough direction for Eli. He knew he'd have to pass the northeast corner where the "Wallendas" worked.

Eli loathed this nickname for the top editors, the ones who supposedly performed a high-wire act at the last minute, deciding what should go into the magazine. Even before its cuteness wore thin, Eli doubted the phrase's accuracy. Far from performing aloft, these editors seemed to spend all their waking hours securing and testing nets.

Through a long glass wall and sooner than he'd expected, Eli saw Nina sitting at her desk. Her office was *in* the Wallendas' corner. Directly opposite his place on the compass, plus twice as long and two floors up.

When Eli walked in, Nina rose from her seat of power and came over to hug him. "I'm so glad you're back. I was so worried about you." She gestured for Eli to sit down on her couch. When he did, she nestled herself in the opposite end.

236

Her eyes were still an innocent baby blue. When they were lovers, they'd once stood naked together in front of his full-length mirror and compared their bodies. They'd just made love and were discussing sex differences—had job discrimination arisen from any physical basis? Giggling like siblings about their different endowments, they'd agreed that they had almost identical color eyes.

Nina's eyes looked as twinkly as ever, but her face had broadened. Whatever professional hold she had on him, he was no longer in her emotional thrall.

"You've lost a lot of weight," Nina said.

"The fright diet."

"You don't look frightening," Nina said, mistaking his meaning. Perhaps he appeared frightful.

When they were breaking up, Nina had shouted, "You don't seduce and abandon. You let yourself *be* seduced and then you muster the strength to pull away. You think *abandonment* is strength." At this moment, she'd delighted him. Like most journalists, Eli sought sources who'd go on the record with his innermost feelings.

"I missed you this past summer," she said. "Not least of all to trade gossip. You've been missing the story of the decade."

"China? Or Eastern Europe?"

"Both, of course. I was also thinking about the Time-Warner merger. Anyway, let's talk about what *you've* been through. Tell me everything."

"Everything?"

Nina looked at her watch. Gold, with a lapis face.

"I'm in no rush."

Eli's mind was racing. He couldn't begin with the goddam dream. Even a woman he'd slept with wouldn't believe him if a nightmare was his tip-off. How should he pitch this story? Every writer at *Newsweek* loathed these first seconds when you either captured your editor's attention or failed.

"I discovered the Pentagon's most advanced research project. It's an incredibly destabilizing weapon."

Incredibly. He regretted introducing this modifier. But at least he was off and running. Smack into Patsy. He couldn't mention her, either. Nina might suspect that he'd slept with her. How could Eli make a righteous pitch when he'd transgressed their profession's most basic ethical line?

"Let me outline what I've discovered about the Air Force's Black Hole." He described the hidden budget figures, Forst's underground plant and Raindrop's nature while monitoring Nina for hints of MEGO — "My Eyes Glaze Over" — the editor's early-warning system for boring stories.

Happily, the flash fire in his cabin aroused Nina's attention. She reached over to clasp Eli's hand. Once he had her sympathy, he didn't want to stretch its limits. He made his sudden trip to Moscow seem primarily adventurous. He tried simultaneously to convince and distract Nina with details: the airport's pre-industrial lights, the lingering diesel smell on Moscow's streets, the ancient passages beneath the Kremlin.

"When Colonel Ulyanova put me on the plane to Tokyo, she tried to embrace me as if she'd never been my jailer." Eli noticed Nina shift slightly—her beige business suit had a silk paisley lining. A woman executive's kimono hiding and displaying hints about her femininity and power. Bergdorf's? Chanel?

Like a news anchor with a wire in his ear connecting him to the control booth, Eli was quite capable of pitching a story while monitoring himself. But now it wasn't just his self-producer telling him what to do. There was an open mike in the control room. He heard simultaneous feeds coming in from all over the world.

Marbles. A Japanese sleeper? Spies studying sports. Delayed fuses. While Eli was describing the test island, Nina withdrew her hand.

"Do you have any questions?" he asked.

"Are you finished?"

How the hell could he be finished? Didn't she want to hear what had happened on the goddam island? "Not quite," he said.

He rushed straight to Marbles' death, then the Big Bang. He omitted Ratu's demise. He'd already tested Nina's limits. Plus Ratu wasn't really relevant. Eli's story was over. He'd merely omitted the beginning, the heart and the end.

"That may be the most incredible tale I've ever heard," she said. "Thank God it's behind you."

Eli saw Powers behind him.

"What would you like to do about it?" she asked.

Do? If Eli had offered to swallow his whole nightmare and return to his pop culture beat, he suspected she would have embraced him. Not that she doubted his veracity. She'd just made a quick calculation: what she and *Newsweek* might gain from this story were outweighed by all the risks and likely repercussions. Who knew (or even cared) how the Big Top audience might react to Eli's virtuoso act? Nina was simply terrified by the absence of nets.

"Write a story about it, of course," Eli said.

"Of course," Nina echoed, throwing up her hands. "I meant: Given the complications of a murder and an attempted murder, no hard evidence, no authoritative sources on the record, your personal involvement and so on, what *kind* of story do you propose writing?"

"I know the rules."

"All right, give it your best shot." Nina said, bouncing up from the couch. She walked back behind her desk and opened her calendar. "I'm not free for lunch tomorrow. Or the day after that. But . . ."

"I'll have a draft for you by 6 o'clock," Eli said, hurrying out of her office.

Eli spent the rest of the day typing into his computer that *Newsweek* had sufficient evidence to deduce that a decade ago, a faction in the military had conceived Star Wars as an offensive system. Under the direction of one Maj. Gen. Wilson Powers, Jr., this cabal had secretly pursued their objective using money buried in the Pentagon's black budget and diverting DOE funds designated for nuclear cleanup. They had extensive, underground R&D facilities in Silicon Valley just east of Lockheed. They'd just successfully (if you call "success" missing by three blocks) completed a test shot from space to a target in the South Pacific. The Black Hole leaders who'd survived their own lethal infighting were now poised to petition the President for a secret roll-out of their system: orbiting nuclear-tipped missiles that could wipe out Moscow's underground military headquarters instantaneously. Should the Communist Party self-destruct, Raindrop would be poised as our weapon to intimidate other militant leaderships in the future.

Eli omitted all his own perils, as well as explicit mention of Marbles' death.

When he'd finished the draft, he gazed up from his computer tube and noticed the new skyscraper's torso had risen high above his floor. He stepped over to his window and peered down through the urban canyon to the building's base. A crane was hoisting thin slabs of marble off of a truck. They were about to put an impressive face on this ordinary building.

The year before last, when the building site was being excavated, Eli had heard whistles warning of the dynamite explosions to come. After a while, he'd become acclimated. He stopped hearing the whistles. Blasts would jolt him out of the blue.

He sat down and reread his draft. All stories were

241

a balancing act—tame enough for editors to handle, yet sufficiently upsetting so that they might have effect. What might jolt the American public? Americans used to think that the Soviets deserved deadly threats; now they were likely to dismiss this poor enemy as unthreatening.

A missile experiment fired down from space might catch the margins of public attention. But what proof could Eli offer? The Pentagon could claim that an ICBM with a dummy warhead had been fired from Vandenberg, routinely exited the atmosphere and returned to test-strike the island Eli had described.

Even the possibility that nuclear weapons might eventually be based in space wouldn't upset the public. Americans were too comfortable to fret about some future threat. They'd balance any potential danger with a belief that the U.S. had to be technologically prepared. Wasn't America the most ethically equipped to be the world's overseer?

Eli rubbed his chest. Had the blast on the island been nuclear? He had no way of knowing. Certainly they were planning for Raindrop to be nuclear. So they might have needed to detonate a tiny warhead underground to prove the weapon's earth penetrating abilities and destructive appeal.

On the other hand, with a nuclear test Powers risked deadly political fallout.

Although Eli wasn't sure about the explosion's nature, *Newsweek's* editors would have no way of checking either. They were likely to challenge him on other points.

He reworked his copy to state: "In violation of international treaties, common decency and public trust, the air force's recent test in the South Pacific was nuclear." Then he called Nina's extension. "A finished draft is in your computer basket. I've slugged it BLHO."

"Blowhole?" she asked.

"Yes," Eli said, simultaneously changing BLHO to "Blowhole." He could accept editing. Wasn't he trying to blow a hole in the Black Hole?

"Terrific," she said. "I'll get back to you shortly."

An hour later she did get back. "Looks interesting. I've sent around copies and have scheduled a meeting in two days at 10 A.M. That will give the Washington bureau some time to check with their sources before they come up."

"The Washington bureau?" Marbles' logic flashed before him. Powers could get to these people.

30

Disinformed

Two days later Eli arrived at the meeting in his gray pinstriped suit. On his newly lean frame, his jacket felt gangsterish. That morning he'd had to punch an extra hole in his best belt and cinch it as tightly as possible.

The room was crowded with emissaries from the Washington bureau. Eli was glad he'd picked out a button-down, Oxford broadcloth shirt. It was the collar of the day.

Somebody else from Washington was still expected. No one seemed particularly upset by the delay. Eli tried to stay calm; he picked up a Danish and edged over to the crowd.

Nina made introductions. If top management had too many Smiths, the Washington bureau was thick with Thomases. In last and first names. Eli felt as if he were at a reunion of a prep school he'd never attended.

Perhaps he was being paranoid. Their conference quarters, after all, were less grand than he'd expected. He'd walked by this interior room several times before, but he'd always assumed the bigwigs had something more impressive at their disposal.

Not that he'd been eager to find out. One reason he stayed in the back of the book—besides the fact that he'd never been asked to join the front—was that he despised meetings. Critics, even pop critics, weren't obliged to forge consensus.

The center of the conversation was a new editor who'd just defected from *Time*. He was detailing cuts in staff, travel, benefits, researchers and expense accounts that his former employer was making to pay the debts incurred merging with Warner. Everyone listened intently as the richer family up the block—the ones who'd taken better trips and had better guests at their parties—was again exposed for what the *Newsweek*s always knew they were: snobs who'd trim standards to maintain their standing.

The final arrival was an Exeter-Harvard-Oxford grad who wrote about arms control. He opened the meeting with a preemptive strike. "My apologies for being late, but I just had breakfast with Scowcroft. He said that no weapon called Raindrop ever existed and that they're continuing to scale back SDI. When I pressed him on this latter point—since I suspected there might be some news here—he said that if one reread Bud McFarlane's Contragate testimony, one would see that from the first the NSC viewed SDI as a negotiating card. Reagan and Weinberger got carried away with Star Wars rhetoric. Even Quayle understands this now. Scowcroft said that he doesn't want to be quoted, even for indirect attribution, because they don't want to alarm the right-wingers. But they plan to keep scaling SDI back to minimal R and D, maybe three billion. At this level, the Soviets will tone down their objections."

The room exhaled an audible ahhh. Scowcroft hadn't only denied what they'd never believed—the national security adviser had also taken breakfast with *them* on short notice.

The Pentagon correspondent spoke up, "That certainly comports with my calls. None of my sources has heard boo about any Black Hole. An assistant undersecretary with DIA connections said that several years ago he heard that the Soviets feared SDI's first strike capabilities. But he stressed that this intercepted traffic was old and suspect. He hinted that the Soviets had probably been using this imagined threat as an excuse to refurbish their deep shelter program. And maybe now, since they're in such desperate straits, they may be laying the seeds of a new disinformation campaign to undermine *glasnost*."

So this was how they were going to dispense with the story, Eli thought: me as dupe.

The bureau chief now spoke. "These are terribly difficult kinds of stories. It's very easy to be misled. As we all know, *Time* was misled just this past summer to exaggerate the extent of a KGB penetration. You may not have seen that, Eli," he said, graciously. "They were forced to print a very embarrassing retraction."

"So," Nina asked Eli in her brightest voice. "What's your response to all this?"

The group's cologne and aftershave had collected into a sweet smell that sickened Eli. "Not to be rude," he said, "but you're all naive."

Naive! Exactly the word they'd been awaiting. Floodgates of abuse opened.

"My God, man, we had a talk on the shuttle up and pooled all of our sources. Not one of them had ever talked to you? Where the hell did your information come from? Left field?

"I doubt it," said another. "The left—I'm talking *New York Review*, McGeorge Bundy—understands that disarmament is for real. Obviously one can question the stability of the Kremlin leadership and the boldness of this Administration. But all sides know we're at an historic moment. There's no turning back."

"Jim Baker understands this timing and the breadth of the disarmament constituency," added *Newsweek*'s man at State. "Even taking the most cynical view of Baker as a master of publicity, he knows all the natural momentum is on our side. He'd never risk such a public relations fiasco."

"And Cheney," the Capital Hill correspondent chimed in, "If you talk to his former colleagues, or Nunn's and Aspin's staffs today, they'll all tell you he's a straightshooter. He knows that Star Wars doesn't have the votes anymore. Cheney's not going to betray Congress. He needs bipartisan support to hold onto the core of his budget. Besides, what you're postulating violates several treaties."

"Do you even read your own magazine?" asked

247

the intelligence correspondent as he held up a clipped "Periscope" section. "We reported this summer that Bill Webster is on the outs because *nothing's happening* at the Agency. They're out of the loop."

Eli surveyed the room: Blessed consensus. And at an interloper's expense. After this meeting, they'd never see him again.

Eli rose and walked to the blackboard. On it was a graph from a previous meeting that listed newsstand sales figures for the past two years. "Dog Intelligence" and "Adam & Eve" were two peaks Eli noticed as he erased. Then he wrote: "NAMES, FIGURES, TECHNOLOGY." Underneath each he outlined details he'd gleaned from the Black Hole. His technological knowledge was sketchy, he realized, but the little he knew made him a rocket scientist compared to these junior diplomats.

"You're saying my story is implausible. It goes against everything your sources tell you. I don't doubt that this is true. Of course your sources regard you as a second tier p.r. agency—a clipping service for what they've leaked the previous week to the *Post* and the *Times*."

"Did you get that on deep background from the former Larry Speakes?" the *Time* refugee asked.

Nasty, nervous laughter all around.

Eli waited until it subsided. "All I'm proposing is that you independently research these names and numbers. Concentrate on Maj. Gen. Wilson Powers, Jr. He's the lynchman. I mean 'linchpin.' I'm prepared to accept your conclusions if you do two honest days' research."

Honest days' research! The audacity. Strictly on a time-clock basis, the Washington bureau punched in more hours than any other *Newsweek* staff.

Before anyone could object, Nina piped up, "That sounds fair enough to me."

"Two days research when we get the chance! We have a weekly to put out."

"Well, this is one story," said the editor-in-chief, who'd been silent until now, "where there's no danger we'll be scooped by *Time*."

Sniggers all around. Eli left the room. Walking down the stairs to his office he felt like a reprimanded teenager. After five minutes, he rang Nina's extension.

"Hello."

"Those fucking idiots," he said.

"How nice to hear from you. I'm tied up right now," Nina said, cheerily. They'd regrouped in her office, where they were probably deriding Eli. "Can I give you a ring back within the hour?"

"You're the boss," Eli said and they both hung up.

She was selling him out. He retreated to his computer and found the "Corporate Restructuring" file. Was it possible for him to take early retirement? Would Powers hunt him down if no story appeared? As he was calculating how much money he could walk away with, Nina appeared at his door.

"I don't remember it being so dark in here," she said.

Eli gestured to his window. "Saks sold its backyard to the Swiss."

"Of course, I'd forgotten. Listen, you were terrific this morning."

"Terrific? I was butchered. Didn't you hear that parting shot?"

"You got off a couple shots of your own. Now it's time to disengage. Take in a picture," Nina said, showing her small town roots. "You're got to recover your professional distance. No story is a matter of life or death."

31

Nuclear Resonance

Just as Eli was about to fall asleep, fire or ambulance or police sirens pierced his ears. The New York night was filled with routine alarms.

The next morning, when he spit his toothpaste back into the porcelain basin, he noticed the white foam was infused with blood. He bared his gums to the mirror—they were inflamed. And brushed again until he realized that the repeated exercise of the brush wouldn't stanch the bleeding.

He grimaced at the mirror: his nightmare had come home.

Escaping to his office, Eli considered what to do if they spiked his story. Marbles was right—neither the *Times* nor the *Post* would pick up on anything that *Newsweek* had published so they certainly wouldn't consider a story that had been rejected.

Go directly to TV? He knew a top producer at *60 Minutes,* but he feared he'd burned this bridge with his Mike Wallace profile. Why had Eli been so hostile? Because in New York, Descartes' proof had been updated: I have a critical opinion, therefore I am. On the attack, New Yorkers felt alive.

Eli didn't feel alive this morning. His bleeding gums, his lack of sleep, the confusion of time zones—he had the bends from ascending so quickly from the deep.

Nina advised him to take in a picture. He'd take her literally. He'd search for that Hopper painting he and Patsy had discussed: The Bridle Path. First he zigged quickly across Fifth to the Museum of Modern Art. No luck. Then he zagged back uptown to the Whitney, checking repeatedly to see if he was being tailed.

The Hopper paintings and sketches on display depicted New York rooftops. Or naked women. Or naked women seen from rooftops. White light streaked diagonally into dark places. Hopper was a Peeping Tom.

Eli peeped around him: No menace apparent. On this Indian summer day, perhaps the last of the season, a few women still sported salsa colors. Very soon New York would shed its Latin summer skin and settle down to the business of business.

Hopper's nudes were unfashionably stocky. They stood solidly alone. The nude in front of him looked as if she'd had her babies and felt no subsequent need to slim down. Eli entered the canvas with the understanding that she shouldn't be touched.

His mind kept blurring, as if he were wearing a goggle mask. He rubbed his eyes with his hands, then stared at his fingers. His nail beds looked ghastly white.

When Eli pulled back his covers that night, he panicked that Powers might again set him aflame. He retreated to his bedroom door with his shoes in hand. As if he were shooting a pair of free throws, he lofted one after another onto his bed. No conflagration.

When he finally lay in bed, unable to sleep, he imagined Patsy in a Hopper. She was gaining substance. Since she was pregnant with his child, why hadn't she called him? Maybe she didn't know he was back, but why wasn't she trying to find out? Did she feel she'd trapped him already?

Eli believed that a man should accept equal responsibility for birth control. Patsy hadn't gotten pregnant by herself; he'd impregnated her. But just as she'd never envisioned marrying a man as rejecting as Powers, Eli had never imagined starting a family without his explicit consent. Had he been trapped or raped?

He laughed at his own perversion. Patsy probably wasn't pressuring him because she wanted him to choose freely. She was classy. Not a patsy, but a patrician. He should start calling her Patricia, even in his own mind.

That this *Patricia* was willing to raise his child alone infuriated him. He didn't want anyone else raising his child. The idea of a fatherless child was unbearable. Fear that he couldn't guarantee his child he'd always be around was precisely what had prevented him from mating all these years. And now the fear had a basis.

This third evening back he was no more acclimated to Manhattan. There were as many sirens as the nights before.

They assembled in the same conference room. Today it seemed airless as well as windowless. The correspondent with the best intelligence contacts began: "A star representing one Frank Marbles has just been engraved on the CIA's north wall. That's where they honor agents 'Who Gave Their Lives In The Service Of Their Country.' One rumor has it that Kremlin hardliners, through overseas agents, might be the culprit."

"Bullshit," Eli uttered. "He was fragged."

The Pentagon correspondent spoke up. "There's an obscure air force line item called 'other production charges.' It matches the FY-'81-FY-'89 figures Franklin claims were spent on Raindrop during the last decade."

"Now we're talking!" Eli said giddily.

"Where did you get your information from?" the Washington bureau chief demanded with the sternness of a headmaster. "I think we have a right to know who's leaked this material to you? What's their agenda?"

"This leak is on no one's agenda," Eli said. "That's why it hasn't made the news."

Eli's persistence pissed them off. They might swallow even Eli's facts so long as he cited an authoritative source. But no veterans present wanted to buy into a story that had come from observation, let alone participation.

The arms control specialist said, "You claim this weapon is General Powers' baby. I've contacted practically everyone in the nuclear priesthood and not a one has heard of this Powers. So who confirmed that this weapon might be nuclear?"

"I saw the test with my own eyes."

"If *that's* true, why are you sitting here instead of seeing a doctor?"

Eli glanced at Nina. She had the same cheery smile pasted on her face. She was going to let this fight play itself out before she stepped in to restore order.

Eli's giddiness deflated in an exhale he could smell. Why had he pushed his personal involvement and the nuclear point? Exhibitionism? Self-destructiveness? He felt nauseated not by the Wasps' cologne, but by his own dread.

"I'd be glad to see a doctor," Eli said. "I've been considering it myself."

A doctor specializing in radiation poisoning was located at Columbia's Physicians & Surgeons. Eli's lymphocytes were sorted into subtypes and counted; his skin inspected for beta burns; his intercellular components analyzed for ionization damage. After examining Eli's eyes, the doctor took a detailed medical history stretching back a full year.

This exceedingly thin physician had nine diplomas on his wall, documenting post-graduate medical work. Either he'd been so enmeshed in his studies

255

that he'd never found time to eat. Or else his studies had led him to believe that all food was poisonous.

Eli's case seemed to trouble the doctor. He scanned Eli's test results twice, then asked, "Are you claustrophobic?"

"No."

"Good, because there's one final test I'd like you to take inside of a small, but extremely sophisticated imaging machine."

"I know about it! I'm . . ." he searched for the right word, ". . . engaged to the woman whose father conceived this machine. Have you ever heard of Wilhelm Geist?"

"I can't say that I have, but you're marrying into an incredible gene pool. This machine spins your protons, then calculates density according to the rate at which they slow down. Echoes from the MRI will show us everything that's inside of you."

For a minute Eli wondered if he could be mistaken. "Is MRI the same as Nuclear Magnetic Resonance?"

"Yes, they've just changed the name because the word 'nuclear' seems to upset a lot of people. In this instance it just refers to the nuclei of atoms inside your body. This machine doesn't emit any radiation. I don't want you to think I'd ever risk adding insult to any injury you've already suffered."

"You've already suffered" echoed afterward. Eli always wanted to witness the worst, but without suffering fatal consequences. He believed that witnessing was preventive medicine. The doctor appeared to be thinking along opposite lines.

Eli went to a special wing dedicated to the giant machine. He was given a light green gown and told to shed all metal from his body. After changing, he entered the machine's sanctum, which was separated from the control booth by a glass wall. In the control booth stood the doctor. If he wasn't worried about Eli, wouldn't he have waited for the test results in his own office?

Into the futuristic sanctum came a tech with a familiar Johnson & Johnson package. He indicated that Eli should lie down on the putty-colored, body-length tray. Then he extracted two wads of cotton and placed them in Eli's ears.

"The machine makes a loud sound," he shouted. "Just ignore it. For the next couple of hours, you shouldn't move a muscle. Try not to swallow. Just relax."

He slid Eli into the MRI's narrow tube.

Eli felt as if he were in a cryonic chamber of a space-age morgue. They were freezing him so that scientists in the future could tell where he'd gone wrong.

A beat jackhammered through the machine. Hammered through Eli. His cells were being sounded. He'd heard that a father might give a prospective son-in-law the once over, but this was a bit extreme.

The temperature started to rise. Lying there in the tubular dark, his arms pressed tight against his side, Eli's thoughts narrowed: Powers wanted to become an invisible absolute, hidden by virtue of his improbability. Americans were loathe to believe that any part of them relished destruction.

Eli felt a sleek anger, as if he'd shaped himself into a lone missile intent on shooting down this hovering enemy. Instinctively he covered his privates.

"Don't move again," a muffled voice ordered through a built-in speaker.

Two hours later, when he'd dressed and put his metal back on, the doctor greeted him. "Do you want to see yourself on your father-in-law's machine?"

The depthful pictures were in black and white. Eli had expected color, like the paintings of the brain beside Patricia's closet door.

"See these grays inside of you," the doctor said, pointing with his yellow pencil along Eli's bones. "They're perfectly normal. If they were mottled, we might have something to worry about. I was a little worried given your other results."

"Why?"

"We really don't understand this stuff yet," the doctor hedged.

"What are you telling me?"

"You show some minor signs of radiation poison, but your body looks as if it's recovering."

"So what don't you understand?"

"Well, you may be developing radiation cataracts. We can easily operate on them. It's just that your eyes and some markers in your blood indicate a pace of poisoning that I haven't seen before. Given the history of dread, weight loss, fever and fatigue you've described, my best guess is that the incident happened some nine months ago. But that's when you say you were living peacefully in California."

He must have been exposed when he was underground in Forst's plant. They must have been doing some forbidden testing in the bowels of that facility. But he'd broken in *six* months ago.

The initial incandescent dream passed before Eli. Impossible.

The third *Newsweek* meeting took place after the doctor forwarded his report. Everyone sat at a discreet distance from Eli. They didn't want to get too close, but they didn't want to disown him, either. He was a bomb that might go off in their midst.

"Obviously you've been exposed to something dangerous, but since none of us knows exactly what, couldn't you write a little more theoretical piece?" asked one top editor.

"Something less *ad hominem?*"

"Maybe add a bit of irony?"

"I'm sure Eli could do that," Nina said.

"Of course," Eli agreed, picking up on her cue. He'd defined the outer limits; he could show how reasonable he was by tacking back a bit.

He returned to his office and called up his draft. Staring at the "Author: FRANKLIN," he remembered how in grade school he'd identified with his namesake Ben. Even as a nine-year-old, he wanted to grasp ideas from the sky *and* impress people with his practicality.

He composed a compromise essay. "Just as the Manhattan Project capped WW II, a new weapon and grand strategy are emerging at the close of the Cold War. The weapon is Star Wars and the strategy is U.S. domination of the planet from space.

"Shortly after Reagan's election, a small group decided that Star Wars could be sold as a Trojan umbrella. President Reagan offered the world a defensive shield that would render nuclear weapons 'impotent and obsolete.' And actually we are building SuperPatriots and other anti-ballistic missiles to help prevent enemy warheads from raining down on us. We're also developing orbital anti-satellite weapons to knock out an enemy's eyes and ears in case *we* decide to strike first.

"With what? Raindrop—the tip of our nuclear umbrella.

"A prototype of this space-based weapon has been created behind the Air Force Space Command's Blue Curtain of secrecy in the Special Access Required 'Black Hole' project. Because the Black Hole's Raindrops are designed to penetrate hardened headquarters, a frustrated American president facing a hardened despot might find their use irresistible. And since Raindrops require only tiny, precisely targeted nuclear warheads, this program can be marketed as efficient disarmament when the public mood is deemed right."

"The irony," Eli wrote, though he hated pointing out ironies, "is that these competitive strategists don't believe even in the possibility of disarmament. Like confirmed Leninists, they feel nations are perpetually at war. Since peace to them is a hypocritical state — merely covert conflict — they're willing to dislodge Gorbachev so that they can face off against an outright antagonist. Or open the Pandora's Box of a Soviet Civil War.

"If another enemy besides the Soviets can be found — say a maniacal Third World dictator — they would be eager to discard thousands of our obsolete ICBMs with great fanfare while secretly channeling our military energy into space.

"With or without the virtue of current enemies, their 21st Century aim is for the US to become the planet's *techno-capo-di-tutti-cappi*, the chief of all chiefs to whom other countries come for insurance before they project force or inflict a little punishment on their neighbors. As an object lesson in the benefits of American protection, we may inflict massive retaliation on those petty dictators previously on our payroll who defy us."

Worried that this prospect might appeal to too many readers, Eli waved the flag. "These hardliners' ill-will toward leaders extends to their own. President Bush should set up an investigatory commission full of patriotic men and women brave enough to excavate the truth. At the very least, since tens of billions are being sucked into the dark, the country deserves an accounting."

Any commission, Eli realized, would be a sham. But at least the President had been served public notice. Defense, the CIA and the National Security Council would have to suffer inquiries. One match had been lit in the dark.

Two hours after Eli passed his revision on to Nina, he called her to ask when they'd have their next meeting.

"No more meetings. Your piece is going through."

"Terrific," he heard himself say in her timbre.

For the next day he spied electronically as his copy was infected with what he called *Newsweasel* words: "nevertheless," "however," "arguably." "The irony is" became "The real irony is." These additions added the illusion of nuance. They gave the sense that this story, like all stories, had many sides. Enough sides so that one could feel informed without having to do anything.

Late Saturday, after closing time, Eli contacted the copy chief and said there was one sentence he needed to rework slightly.

He cut out one line and added his *hominem:* "The Colonel North of this diabolical project is Maj. Gen. Wilson Powers, Jr."

For just a second Eli wanted his audience to co-exist with him in a world where evil had a common name.

He shipped his copy back and waited anxiously for someone to object. When midnight approached, he realized: In a day General Powers would confront his story.

32

Unexpected Turbulence

Monday morning, Eli found "Disarmament's Dark Side?" in the final two columns of *Newsweek*'s International section on page 42. They'd tinted his story's background with gray so that it appeared to be some sort of sidebar. And placed it on a left-hand page opposite a Sears' advertisement for "The Best Value in Treadmills." This was the kind of tacky retail ad that usually occupied less favorable magazine real estate in the very back of the book.

The phone rang.

"Mr. Franklin, Bart Rougemont from National Public Radio. Quite an intriguing piece you've written. Might we chat about it for *All Things Considered* in about an hour?"

"Sure."

"I'll call you back then."

After hanging up, Eli reread his article. It did contain General Powers' name and harsh accusations, especially if one knew how to read between the lines.

Between Eli's space and the elevator was an office occupied by the senior science writer. A scholarly fellow with a Ph.D. in the history of science from Princeton. Eli now rose and meandered past his neighbor's open door.

"Hello, Eli, I haven't seen *you* in a long time." No compliment. He hadn't read Eli's piece.

"I've been working on something that's in the front of the book this week."

"Really! I'll have to read it today. I'm not a big fan of the puff they usually run up there."

"Neither am I." Eli leaned casually against the doorjamb. "Hey, I've been meaning to ask: Have you ever heard of Wilhelm Geist?"

"Of course, he's a big name. Just a notch below Einstein and Heisenberg. A visionary. When I was at Princeton, he spent a year at the Institute for Advanced Studies."

"No kidding."

"Would you like to borrow some books I have discussing his work?"

"I'd like to," Eli said, "although it's his family that really interests me. You wouldn't have any reason to know about them, would you?"

"There was some gossip about his wife."

"Which was?"

"She'd died the year before he visited. Apparently she was even brighter than her husband, but given to black periods. Still, rumors aren't to be trusted."

"Get to the point, friend: Was the gossip that she'd killed herself?"

"I believe. Is that your phone?"

Eli hurried back to his office. "Hello. Hello."

264

Someone listened, then hung up. Probably not Joan Baez. A minute later the phone rang again. "Yes."

"Congratulations!" It was Nina. "Your story is playing well."

"You heard about NPR?"

"Are they doing something?"

"Just a little interview."

"I'm not surprised. You deserve credit."

Why this surge in support. "Where have you heard the story is playing well?"

"Also in Washington. But don't ask me for any details because I'm still checking. I should know something later today. Can I interest you in dinner?"

"Sure."

"Then let's make it eight at the Cafe des Artistes. I've moved into that building so I'll meet you in the lobby."

When the NPR correspondent called back, he told Eli that the Pentagon and the CIA had refused comment, saying that the accusations in Eli's story were so out of the mainstream, they were clearly absurd. The White House had issued a curt denial stating that it knew of no such weapons program.

The interview with NPR was so friendly Eli was surprised by how quickly it ended. Soon afterward, a curious reporter called from *The Philadelphia Inquirer*. In the past, Eli might have cautiously traded information. Today he decided to dump. The *Inquirer* was as good a place as any — it had found a niche as a paper of journalistic record where reporters could file long stories for Pulitzer consideration. Eli detailed everything he knew without revealing his personal involvement. The more widespread his story, the safer his person.

He waited in his office to hear *All Things Considered*. Teased as "Contragate in Space?" his interview came during the show's final half hour. Rougemont's edit had eliminated a few facts and increased the friendliness. The segment had its own conspiratorial tone.

Afterward Eli waltzed across town to meet Nina at 1 West 67th, a fancy building that bordered Central Park. The prices in this inner core of Manhattan were prohibitive. She had to be making twice his salary, at least.

As he waited in the lobby, the early dinner crowd exited toward Lincoln Center. Nina emerged from the elevator wearing a lapis shirtwaist dress. The maître d' escorted them into a room whose walls were painted with nude nymphs cavorting in the woods. These murals were evocative not just of sex, but of a time when urban suggested urbane, not decay.

"Order anything you want," Nina said. "Dinner's on the company."

Nina's necklace was made of oversized faux pearls. Her hair was sculpted to suggest spontaneity. Eli couldn't immediately place the look.

"So what was the word you heard from Washington?" he asked.

"Smith played coy. But it must have been nice

enough because he's started to own your story a bit."

"Which might mean?"

"Maybe Kay Graham said something pleasant to him in passing when she was reviewing this week's magazine."

"Will the *Post* do a follow-up?"

"Doubtful. Mrs. Graham gave up control years ago. Her son is just waiting for Bradlee to pass on so he can run his own show. Not that I expect changes. Each year the *Post* plays a more conservative role in the permanent government."

Nina ordered a bottle of expensive bordeaux. As she tasted her gravlax appetizer, Eli asked, "Why don't they just call themselves the U.S. Department of the *Washington Post?*"

"You always had a way with images."

"What does that make our outlet—the Voice of America?"

"Now don't underestimate New York's cultural clout. Because this last piece of yours was based in D.C., we had to endure a little turf battle. But you can freely gore other sacred American cows. Or celebrate those who've risen above the herd."

Nina's new look came into focus: *Vanity Fair*. And Eli realized that the attitude problem of his that he'd feared was actually anti-attitude and not really a problem. He asked, "Are the early retirements finished at our place?"

"Another thing I wanted to discuss. There's going to be a little restructuring down on your floor and

267

the office in the northeast corner may open up. You'd get a better view up Madison than I have. You'd be sitting atop St. Patrick's."

"Actually, Nina, I was wondering if I could still qualify for the plan."

"Just what I had feared! Why do you think I'm making you these offers? Just when you might begin to become a player, you want to quit. Aren't you sick of that pattern?"

"Nina, I need to go back to California."

"There's a woman out there, I knew it."

"We're in the middle of a risky relationship. I don't know her as well as I should. But my gut tells me that it will work out. It has to."

Nina went on calmly with her meal. Since *Newsweek* had erred in placing Eli on involuntary leave, they owed him some pay. She'd give him six months' of benefits if he'd do occasional stringer work. Then he'd return to Manhattan, she was sure.

Afterward, in the lobby, she asked, "Do you want to see my new apartment?"

Her brassiness was a turn-on. He kissed her and she tightened their embrace beyond old friendship.

"I'm not proposing marriage," she said. "I have no more desire to be tied down than you do."

He kissed her again, then he sauntered away up Broadway to his co-op, where he called Patricia.

"This is Patricia Geist. I'm not home . . ."

"This is Eli. I'm back. I love you. I'm dying to see you and our baby. I'll tell you everything tomorrow night as soon as my flight arrives."

The next morning, he called her again. Her answering machine. Odd that she'd be out late and so early the next morning. He gave her machine his flight details. Then he phoned his brother. Eli hadn't wanted to call him either for fear of alerting Powers.

No one was at his brother's house. Strange. He left a message saying he was returning with a permanent souvenir: himself.

Then he called back the P&S doctor with a question he was embarrassed he hadn't asked before: "Assuming that I was exposed to radiation just before impregnating someone, would the baby suffer any effects?"

"As I said, we're still in the infancy of this science. Were a pregnant woman exposed, the fetus would certainly be at great risk. A man might suffer infertility. But with low-level radiation, we just don't know. An effect called hormesis can actually enhance reproductive capacity. Sometimes in China they radiate seeds before they're planted."

Eli phoned his brother and left another message. "P.S. Remember my promise never to leave you in the dark again? Well, you should know that I've started my own nuclear family."

He spent the rest of the day interviewing brokers and putting his co-op on the market. Then he boarded a United DC-10 bound for San Francisco.

What was the worst he could conceive about Patricia? That she'd conspired with him to take their common trauma to the edge of recapitulation:

they'd created a child who was at risk of being abandoned. He wouldn't let that happen.

As he was relaxing in his seat, he noticed the stewardess from first class whisper something to the stewardess in the business section, who then brought word to the cabin crew in back. Eli casually asked his stewardess, "What was that message?"

"Nothing to worry about."

Her dismissive tone disturbed him. He walked to the head stewardess, who was in the galley adjacent to first class. He said, "I'm a pilot myself and I was wondering: Is there anything wrong with this plane?"

She was a dyed-to-the-roots champagne blonde capable of handling wealthy drunks. "You know every plane has two independent back-up systems for every gizmo."

"So which gizmo have we lost?"

"One of his inertial navigations."

"Inertial or inertia?"

"You're supposed to be the pilot, honey. Why don't you get some sleep? We'll be on the West Coast in no time."

She disappeared behind the curtain into first class.

Eli returned to his seat, cursing that he'd reserved it under his real name.

Powers' name was in national print. If he blew up this plane, the public might scream, "My God, not another DC-10!" United would have to phase these wide bodies faster than they'd already planned. Still, the National Transportation Safety Board would do a detailed autopsy. Even *Newsweek* would be suspicious. Powers wasn't stupid.

But why hadn't Patricia answered? And his brother?

How badly had Eli hurt Powers? Had he made the Black Hole project disappear? Probably he'd forced it further into the dark, where it would fester. Support might be harder to enlist for a while. Powers best hope was to vanish for a few years.

Eli looked around at all the drinking and reading passengers. No, even Powers wasn't this vicious.

Eli wrapped himself in a gray blanket as the flight encountered turbulence.

33

Parting Shot

When he brushed back the curtain separating him from first class, he encountered a door warning "For Players Only." In a dream. He'd discover what was happening on the plane when he awoke.

He opened the door to find the Lakers' locker room pulsing with Aretha's "Respect." Magic sat wrapped in a towel. "My man," Magic said, "you played unconscious."

Eli walked past Magic into the showers. He'd already stripped off his own clothes.

Played unconscious — the ultimate black compliment.

Across from him another player was showering. Andy Lamkin. What the hell was Lamkin doing here?

Flooded with guilt, Eli apologized. "Hey, you made all the key assists. I should have given you the byline."

"Credit is immaterial," Andy said sweetly through the mist.

"Not if you've got a hero complex."

"You've got a bigger problem. Anyway, now's the time to start imagining your kid."

"You know about that?"

"I stay in touch through my wife. She's intense."
Andy left the shower and put on a rose-colored robe.
Because Andy didn't towel off, his robe started to drip
blood.

Eli awoke sweating in his blanket. He rushed forward to the head stewardess. "How are we doing?"

"We're doing fine. But you look like you . . ."

"Have seen a ghost?"

". . . could use a free drink."

"Thanks, anyway," Eli said. He walked back to the
tiny bathroom, where he sobered himself with
splashes of cold water.

He swore he'd contact Andy's wife soon. Explain to
her what had happened. Anyone else might have been
daunted by this task, but tracking down Inez gave
Eli's brain something to chew. Had Powers bought the
Lamkin house to get Inez out of the country? Paid
cash to avoid a paper trail?

Even if Eli didn't excavate evidence incriminating
Powers, he'd locate Inez's forwarding address. Then
he'd visit her in person. If she heard Andy had been
murdered, she'd be even more furious, but her anger
wouldn't be directed at Andy.

The light came on asking all passengers to return to
their seats. When they landed, scattered applause
broke out. Eli wasn't the only nervous one aboard.

Disembarking, he thought about calling Patricia,
but was distracted by a headline in tomorrow's *New
York Times,* whose national edition was already in
the airport's newsboxes. "SDI Shouldn't Be Hurdle in
Disarmament Talks, Bush Says." The President had
given the *Times* an exclusive Oval Office interview to

273

sidetrack Eli's Raindrop story before it gained momentum. With no stenographers or aides present, Bush implied that Star Wars had been confined to mere research on ground-based interceptors and Brilliant Pebbles. The President claimed that he and Gorbachev had agreed to disagree on the future of SDI, which wasn't receiving the Congressional support it deserved anyway.

The transparent remained unexposed. Without a question, Star Wars was going into hiding with a dozen different R&D aliases. For the meantime, only its embattled Soviet targets were in the know. Other targets would be informed in the next century when they threatened American interests.

When Eli reached the baggage area, his suitcases were already circulating on the carousel. His car was still in short-term parking. He scoured through the trunk, under the hood and beneath the chassis for anything suspicious. All he spied were dozens of tiny white chalk marks on his left rear tire. He'd have to pay the garage a fortune. If he wiped off the chalk and claimed he'd lost his ticket, the most they'd charge him for was two days.

"A marked man," he mocked and drove to the exit gate. The bill came to $624.

"What's the largest tab you've ever seen?" Eli asked.

"You're looking at it," the attendant said.

The miles south on 101 elapsed slowly. Industrial complexes and multiplex cinemas, sporting goods supermarkets and endless mini-storage lockers told Eli he was entering Silicon Valley. Other communities around the world dreamed of creating their own high-tech wonderlands, which they imagined to be enlightened work parks generating pure profit and goodwill. Meanwhile in the actual Valley, where workers created subsystems whose applications they dared not imagine, everyone dreamed of escaping but never found the time to live.

Eli tested the 10-mile limit above the speed limit while checking his rearview mirror for police. A car several lengths back kept pace.

Eli slowed down and moved to the middle lane. The friend in his mirror followed. Its piercing yellow floodlights alerted him that this might be Powers.

He switched to the slow lane and turned on his emergency blinkers. The lights behind disappeared into his blind spot. When Eli swiveled his head leftward to make a positive identification, the general's car sped away.

Asshole!

Had Eli's heart stopped beating? His hands were trembling. He punched off his emergency blinkers and regained speed. He wouldn't be intimidated by this bully. He was going to stand by his family whatever threats they suffered.

He exited up University past ranch-style, pseudo-Moorish mansions. Ordinarily he would have approached Patricia's house from the northeast, but he rerouted now so that he came in from the southwest. The general's customized Toyota was nestled near the corner.

Eli rammed its rear and jumped out. He grabbed the general's door handle: Locked.

"C'mon out, insect."

The windows were even darker than Eli remembered. Wraparound limousine-tint. Eli pressed his face against the glass. He couldn't see anyone inside.

He snapped the black metal wipers off the front of the car and whacked away at the windshield. "I know you're in there, you fucking coward. C'mon out of your hardware. Try to murder me with your own hands."

A light flicked on a couple of houses away. Eli turned to see Patricia opening her door. With the fury of 10,000 engines, the Toyota roared away.

Eli ran to Patricia, who welcomed him into the open arms of her rose-colored robe.

"I thought I heard someone yelling," she said after their embrace.

"Your husband playing stalker," Eli said, dropping the wipers he noticed he was still clutching. The rubber blades had left a deep red crease across his fingers.

"God, he's such a two-faced menace. When he came by yesterday, he said, 'I regret we'll never see each other again.' But he said it with vicious sincerity. I should have known he was lying."

"Why did he come?"

"He dropped by unannounced. I was sure he was going to beat me."

"Did he hit you?"

"He pulled out our divorce papers. Then he made a big show of signing them as if he were at an international conference."

"Perfect. His idea of a peace summit. We'd better go inside before General Millennium reappears."

She ushered him into the safety of her bedroom, where Eli asked her to shed her disturbingly rose robe. In her diaphanous nightgown, she looked plump as a pear. "You're radiant," he said, touching her belly.

"When I was lying here alone so frightened for you, I'd rub my belly and reassure myself: 'Life is growing on its own inside me. Eli will be OK. Good things happen naturally.' "

"I'd love to believe that. I may need your help."

"I *want* to help you. I *never* want to be frozen out again."

"I won't do that. I'm proposing the opposite." Eli kissed her softly. He'd forgotten that she smelled like apricots. He savored the aroma and caught another scent as well: A volatile oil streaming from the bathroom. He finished the kiss, then followed his nose. Switching on the light, he found an aquarium on a workstand in her large tub. The aquarium's glass walls had been painted with tiny fish.

"I started an art project when you were away," Patricia called from the bedroom.

The bathroom's white sink was also teeming with painted electric fish, green and blue-eyed creatures evoking Patricia and Eli. On the sink's edge, precisely where El had lifted the general's fingerprints, Patricia had etched a black crab.

"I got a little carried away," she added.

With a burst of talent she'd illuminated the underwater world. Eli stood in awe, thinking: No wonder men venture to black holes.

"So did you get your story?" she asked.

"I did the best I could." Eli came back to the bed.

"Let me tell . . ." Did he hear something? He excused himself again to check the street and the yard. He'd detected the start of a drizzle. He remembered when he'd first fled outside, fearing an earthquake. The rain wasn't refreshing.

He double-locked the doors and secured the windows, then returned to tell Patricia his complete tale. From the first, she was shocked by everything and surprised by nothing. He trusted her enough to confess all his fears and rage.

"My poor baby," she said. Will twists everything around him so that *he* seems normal. He brings everyone's murderous feelings to the surface, then he watches while you boil in your own juices."

"Before he sits down to dine." Eli laughed. As he continued to unravel his story, he was haunted by bursts of dark laughter and inexplicable shame.

It didn't matter. Although Patricia and he were lying beside each other on the bed, Eli felt held. And shivery. And as if having one person really hear his story was more satisfying than capturing the world's attention.

After he was finished, they made love with intimate abandon. Eli worried about hurting their baby *in utero,* but Patricia harbored no such fears. Her pregnancy made her even more full-blooded. She was an enveloping lover. Eli found himself safe in her limbs. His twitchiness subsided. He was swimming beside her, then inside her with the smoothest of strokes. When they came together, pleasure exploded to his extremities, blacking out his brain.

She fell asleep in his arms and he almost did in

hers. Gradually he disengaged. Some minutes later he turned to one side, then the other. Putting his hand under the pillow, he discovered a tightly folded wad. It was opaque white, with his name on it.

He cracked the colorless wax seal and unfolded the paper. Exposed to the light, the type began to disappear as Eli read:

Your article neglected to mention my promotion. Poor Marbles got his star and I got mine. You also didn't mention Ratu's murder. Modesty?

Now that we understand each other, you'll appreciate why I'm no longer in a rush. We can both enjoy the apparent peace until the mood of the country shifts in my direction.

While you've gained a temporary advantage, the seeds of your destruction are gestating. After tonight you won't see me. But your little world will be devastated the moment you suspect I've vanished for good.

Epilogue

September 1991

Eli was reexposed to the rest of the world on a Friday morning. Sterile tent unzipped, he sat Buddha-like on his bed in the isolation ward of Stanford Hospital. He was bald and gaunt. After blasts of chemotherapy and a bone marrow transplant, he'd suffered weeks of vomiting. For too long a time his white blood count hovered at .1. Even that, he was sure, was a wishful fiction. The analytic instruments couldn't register zero, didn't believe zero.

Eli believed it. He'd been at the point of no return. Any earthly contamination would have plunged him over the edge. Teetering he'd made a choice. What pulled him back was a private resolution.

On the TV perched above the foot of his bed, Lucy was scheming with Ethel. In the screen's inset window, delegates to the U.N.'s special session on nuclear, biological and chemical disarmament were convening. Eli enlarged the window — delegates politely milled around the Security Council like guests at an international cocktail party hosted by Scandinavians.

Then the President tapped his gavel, the chatter ceased and all hurried to their places. Eli caught a glimpse of Ulyanova wearing her trademark scarf and suit, this time ashen. She looked smaller than he'd remembered.

The session's first week consisted of alphabetized acclamations of anti-Saddamism. Yesterday the S's and half of the T's had declared their nations' inherently benign natures. As Turkey's speech screeched along Eli's nerves, he imagined Deputy Chief Delegate Powers' impatience.

Eerily, while on the verge of obliteration, Eli had found himself inhabiting the general's skin. During Desert Shield and Storm, he knew the real game plan from the get-go, then anticipated precise military moves before they happened.

Eli sensed that he was occupying a corner of the general's mind as well. Immediately after the cease-fire, *Newsweek* had been leaked a battle narrative from the Air Force Command Center in Riyadh nicknamed the "Black Hole." Their subsequent cover story on "The Secret History of the War" repeatedly highlighted this Black Hole, effectively obliterating Eli's exposé of the real Black Hole in these same pages.

The TV camera scanned the Security Council's horseshoe of seats. Powers' chair was vacant. He must be waiting for the U.S.'s turn to make his appearance.

Eli flipped back to Lucy, who was being chased round and round a table by Ricky. Apparently, inevitably, her scheming had failed.

One of Eli's nurses entered through the sterile anteroom. "This should go down easier," she said, placing a bowl in front of him. She peeled back a thick plastic seal to reveal applesauce.

Eli managed a smile. As compassionate as all of his nurses were, Eli didn't like to engage any of them. Engagement forced him to travel through his body. He'd survived this past month by retreating to a dark space inside where pain couldn't touch him. He'd beat his retreat while his doctors debated whether Eli was suffering from a new kind of radiation exposure or genetically driven leukemia or some combination that would becalm their board-certified confusion.

Eli knew that he'd been exposed to the nuclear shock wave of the future. Not only were the U.S.'s elite warriors testing space-based offensive weapons guided by self-sufficient brains encased in ultratough shells meant to penetrate hardened shelters, they were also experimenting with neo-neutron bombs that specifically targeted the human core. Why not push every edge of the possible? Fifty years from now, in the middle of the 21st century, such a weapon might be necessary. Necessary or not, it would be used.

The applesauce blossomed in his mouth like poisoned fruit. As he shed one body and tried on another (his brother's marrow seemed to be working, but wasn't a perfect fit), he came to realize in every crucified cell that the subtext of all pleasure was pain. From this pitch-black perch, he also realized that good depended upon the existence of evil. No millennium was imaginable without the threat of apocalypse.

He swallowed. The sauce passed down his esopha-

282

gus like flotsam along a river of blood.

Lucy had given way to an animated G.1. Joe. Or Joes. Men and women, a multi-racial crew, fought bad guys distinguished by mustaches and sneers. Both the heroes and their enemies talked in the same mechanical way — their mouths opened and shut in crude time with the dialogue.

If Eli had let himself expire — and nothing would have been easier — he would have succumbed as a cartoon figure. He realized this better than anyone else. One-dimensionality was the keenest pain from which he begged release.

Eli heard Patricia and D.J. enter the anteroom. She was warning him not to play with the betadyne antiseptic scrubber.

Eli flipped the G.1. Joes into the inset window and brought the U.N. onto the main screen. When Eli told Patricia about flirting with death, she became furious. It was the first serious rift in their post-reunion relationship. With a child finally in her hands, she'd lost all patience with the death wish. She didn't find Eli's darkest humor amusing.

Yet oddly, accepting his insignificance released almost superhuman strength. If Eli wasn't responsible for permanently extinguishing Evil, then all his failures (real and imagined) might not carry such a high price. There was no excuse not to rise from the dead and risk a preemptive strike. He'd join hands with others who'd grasped Powers' snuff-or-be-snuffed rule.

Tiny D.J. burst into the room wearing an oversized gown and booties, his bright orange hair poking out from his surgical cap.

"Don't touch your father!" Patricia shouted after him. D.J dashed straight for the control box umbilically tied to the hospital bed.

Eli raised his hand as if to say it was okay. Simultaneously, the foot of the bed began to rise. When Eli's toes pointed to the TV, he noticed that the United States had begun to speak.

Eli pointed to the screen: "Your husband."

Patricia cast a contemptuous glance, then removed the remote control from Eli's hands.

"I have only one husband," she said, shutting off the power. "And he needs to focus on his own recovery."

* * *

General Powers inserted the key into the hidden elevator switch that allowed him to ride down from his penthouse suite to the health club floor. The U.N. Plaza's club officially closed at 10 P.M.. When Powers was forced to overnight in this devil-infested city — the Security Council's disarmament charade was dragging on for months and months — he waited half an hour for the club to be cleaned and cleared. Then he descended to work out in peace.

The $4800 the government was paying weekly for his suite gave the hotel an ample return. Had they quarreled when he asked for his own club key, he was prepared to punish them by checking out immediately and declaring the hotel off limits for the entire delegation.

Because he could negotiate in the dark better than anyone else he knew, Powers went straight to the sauna without flicking on the lights. He turned the thermostat up full blast, then strode to the Cybex room. Three complete sets at 16 minutes per.

Before entering the sauna for good, he poured a couple of cups of water onto the stones to goose the temperature. Then he took a drink for himself from the American Eagle cooler. The water had an acrid aftertaste, as if he'd just swallowed his own sweat.

He lay down on the sauna's upper bench, raised his knees and began doing his sit-ups. He was irritated by sudden stomach cramps. He'd never suffered such a wimpy symptom before. At the count of 42, his heart was hatcheted in half. All color drained from his face. An icy electric chill shrieked back and forth across his upper body.

Anyone else would have panicked. At least paused for several seconds to figure out what was happening. But Powers lived in a state of red alert. He lifted his fist as high as he could, then let it drop on his chest. He repeated this twice. He still couldn't breathe. He swung his numb legs onto the lower bench and lurched toward the sauna door.

It creaked open, then slammed shut. Someone was bracing his body against it!

Rising enough so that his pale face pressed against the inside glass, Powers saw a black masked figure on the other side. Resolute eyes peered out of the two holes.

Powers sunk to the duckboards, then crawled to the sauna's stove. Without pause, he reached in and grabbed a scalding rock. No wince, no sigh.

"Please," he cried out, cocking the hot rock behind his head in the hope that his assailant would expose a moment of weakness.

When the door didn't budge, Powers hurled the rock at the window. It caught a corner and cracked the glass. Immediately a black-gloved hand smothered the hole.

Powers grabbed another rock and lay back on the duckboards, all the while reassuring himself that this was a ruse. The second that this fool thought that anyone could kill General Powers, he would launch a lethal counterattack.

Adam Selassie, the morning attendant, opened the club at a quarter to six. He was greeted by a putrid stench.

"Fucking rich kids," he muttered, jogging toward the sauna. A proud Ethiopian exile, he worked 12-hour shifts just to survive in Manhattan. Last month it was the Hong Kong brats who'd urinated in the sauna, forcing him to flush it out for hours with detergent. Yesterday it must have been the born-rich-again Kuwaitis. Their embassy was right next door.

Perhaps because he was sniffing up the wrong tree, Selassie's first reaction upon seeing the stiff, blue body was guilt. He dragged the dehydrated but warm corpse into the shower room and doused Powers' still-smoldering hand with a bucket of water. Then he called the front desk.

Although the hotel was within spitting distance of

the heavily guarded U.N., the police took their time. This wasn't a death-in-progress. They noted the cracked glass, but weren't quick to make a federal case of it. Stricken men do desperate things.

From a professional standpoint, the general's death was a botched job. Traces of super-potassium were found in his system. Still, given the absence of a motive, his death was listed as a heart attack following exertion. A copy of the coroner's report was sent to the State Department with a cover letter requesting information and inviting inquiries.

If any further investigation took place, it happened behind closed doors and in silence. Vigilant enemies concluded that Powers' project was so well launched, it no longer needed his particular supervision.